P9-EGL-727

An
Unattended
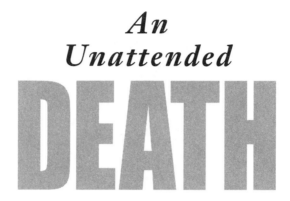

VICTORIA JENKINS

An
Unattended

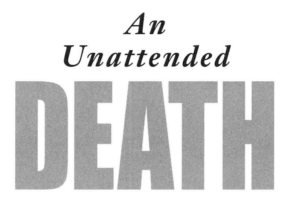

THE PERMANENT PRESS
Sag Harbor, NY 11963

Copyright © 2012 by Victoria Jenkins

All rights reserved. No part of this publication, or parts thereof, may be reproduced in any form, except for the inclusion of brief quotes in a review, without the written permission of the publisher.

Grateful acknowledgement is made for permission to use the following previously published material:

Excerpt from "Highway Patrolman" by Bruce Springsteen. Copyright © 1982 Bruce Springsteen (ASCAP). Reprinted by permission. International copyright secured. All rights reserved.

Excerpt from "Looking Back To See" by Maxine Brown. Copyright © reproduced by The University of Arkansas Press. Reprinted by permission.

For information, address:
The Permanent Press
4170 Noyac Road
Sag Harbor, NY 11963
www.thepermanentpress.com

Library of Congress Cataloging-in-Publication Data

Jenkins, Victoria–
    An unattended death / Victoria Jenkins.
        p. cm.
    ISBN 978-1-57962-284-8
        1. Women detectives—Washington (State)—Fiction.
    2. Murder—Investigation—Fiction. I. Title.

PS3560.E514U53 2012
813'.54—dc23   2012016405

This is a work of fiction. Names, characters, places, and incidents either are the product of the author's imagination or are used fictitiously. Any resemblance to actual persons, living or dead, events, or locales is entirely coincidental.

Printed in the United States of America

To the memory of Jim Crumley,

mentor and friend

I

The body, face down and almost completely submerged in the tea-colored water of the slough, might easily have been mistaken for a driftwood log.

The slough was shallow, less than an acre in size, its irregular banks fringed with reeds. Salt grass grew on a low dune that separated the slough from the Sound, and wild plum thickets and blackberry brambles crowded the inland edges. To the north a stately row of Lombardy poplars delineated the border where the wild Paris land adjoined the Guevara estate.

Underground springs fed the slough and the runoff emptied into the Sound through a narrow channel that cut the dune and ran down the beach into a muddy delta. But at high tide the sea rose and salt water flowed up the channel and into the slough and mingled with the fresh water. During winter storms waves swept over the top of the dune carrying logs and debris.

It seemed odd and implausible that the tides and waves of an August squall would carry a human body from the Sound into the slough. Odd but not impossible. Yesterday evening there had been a squall.

⚜

THESE WERE thoughts in Irene Chavez's mind early on an August Sunday as she stood in the stubble at the bottom of the Paris orchard where someone had cut the grass and pruned an opening through the prickly wild plum, creating a vista of the slough and the Sound and the snowcapped Olympic Mountains beyond, for anyone looking north from the windows of the Paris house above.

No conclusions, she admonished herself. No conclusions. An unattended death was all. Anything could have happened. It could have happened in any way. There could be salt water in the lungs or fresh water or no water at all. There could be a blow to the head or a gunshot wound. It could be a heart attack or a choking incident or hypothermia. Could be suicide or a drug overdose. Death might have occurred in the slough or in the Sound or somewhere else altogether. She must wait and keep an open mind.

The body was almost completely still, just the slightest gentle rocking movements as ripples lapped against it. A flock of wood ducks, lifting off noisily as Irene and Rosalie Paris approached, had left the water momentarily disturbed. Wood ducks, thought Irene, flying south. So soon. Still August. An early sign of fall.

The slough was like a hologram, you could register either the skin of the water, a silvery mirror of the sky, or with a tilt of the head you could look through to what lay beneath. It was shallow, perhaps no more than three feet deep, four in places, and the bottom appeared weedy and muddy and coated with a rusty fur of algae and decaying plant material. The body was just beyond the reeds, face down, just below the surface.

Irene was certain it was a body, something dead and inert, but she was going to have to go in, grapple it to shore, check for vital signs and perhaps attempt resuscitation while she waited for the paramedics. She would prefer not to disturb the scene.

⟞⟝

IT WAS unusual for Irene to be first on such a scene. The county was large and usually when a call came in to 911 volunteer fire-fighters were the first responders. Well-intentioned citizens with no comprehension of preserving evidence.

Mason County covered the southwestern quadrant of Puget Sound, an area that encompassed parts of the Olympic Mountains as well as the islands and isthmuses and peninsulas of the South Sound. Along the shores of the Sound two-lane highways made long meanders around bays and estuaries, often adding miles and hours to distances between points which might be only minutes apart by boat or as the crow flies.

Irene had been southbound on Highway 3 when she heard the dispatch, and she swung left onto Pickering Road and headed for the bridge and Gustavus Island.

⚜

Rosalie Paris had been talking the entire time. She had started talking as soon as Irene's unmarked Crown Vic glided down the driveway with the grill lights flashing and Irene got out. Rosalie had called it in.

"I just was going for some blackberries for my scones," she said in an urgent whisper. "Everybody's still asleep but I was going to make scones—I do almost every morning—and I thought I'd put some blackberries in. These are the big seedy Himalayas, not the early sweet native ones, those are gone now." Pulling Irene along with a hand on her sleeve. "But who cares. They ripen late here. The blackberries down on the edge of the slough are only now getting ripe. We always go across to Long Branch which faces west, you know, so it gets more afternoon sun—there they're ripe in July, the blackberries, and we always have expeditions across. A flotilla, we call it. All sorts of boats go. The canoe, the I-14—that's my husband's sailboat—and the Strausses down the beach have a skiff with an outboard. Libby has a rowing shell and there are kayaks. And there's swimming, which is better on that side for some reason." She paused, then added, "I don't swim, you understand, you couldn't pay me to put on a suit." Rosalie laughed and Irene threw her a glance. An interesting revelation which Irene stored for future reference.

Rosalie, or Rosie as she had quickly amended, in jersey Capri pants under a baggy sweatshirt, attire she might have slept in, would have been pretty once in slimmer, blonder days.

"And blackberry picking," she went on, continuing her thought. "But anyway, now, in August—halfway through August, wow! Already. The summer just whizzes by—now is when the Paris blackberries are ripe." She looked quickly at Irene. "I only need a few. Just a handful. No one minds."

An odd comment. "No, I shouldn't think," Irene said.

"Anne makes jam," said Rosie by way of explanation, "every year. Pints and pints and pints. She pulls an all-nighter just before leaving for home. Actually it's fun. We all stay up and help, or watch, really. The kitchen windows all steam up. She puts a lot of lemon in and not much sugar. For scones I only need a few blackberries, a handful," she said, going on, "so it doesn't matter. No one would notice or care. But if anyone were awake I would have asked at the house as I went past. I looked in the kitchen window but I could tell no one was stirring. It wasn't that early, but they sleep late. I never do."

Listening to Rosalie's parenthetically detailed account of how it was she came to be picking blackberries at seven o'clock on a Sunday morning in August at the bottom of her father-in-law's orchard on a remote island in the southern part of Puget Sound, and how in the course of a kind of Aesopian attempt to reach a particularly enticing cluster she happened to see the body rocking gently against the reeds at the edge of the slough, Irene was at the same time thinking her own thoughts about the process of investigation, which was only now beginning, and beginning to formulate the report that she would give to her superior, Inspector Gilbert, when he arrived.

"I hope it's no one we know," said Rosalie.

"What makes you think it's someone you know?" asked Irene.

"I don't think that," said Rosie, "I didn't say that. I said I hope it's not. You can't really tell anything from here."

"No," agreed Irene. The voluble Rosalie, she thought, whose flood of information suggested utter candor and even idiocy, might actually be the scatterbrain she seemed or perhaps not, perhaps dumb like a fox. Either way she was interesting.

Irene heard dogs faintly, a distant cacophony inland towards the center of the island, and then the sirens that must have set them off: The aid truck and fire engine responding from the volunteer station on the county road that bisected the island north to south along a section line. Now, she thought, she wouldn't have to wade in for the body after all, she'd wait for the EMT personnel who would no doubt have a gaff or a grappling hook. She had not wanted to start the day wet to the waist.

"Ms. Paris," Irene said, laying a hand on Rosalie's arm to interrupt the effusion of anecdote, "you might go back up, if you would, and show them the way."

Silenced, Rosalie listened for a moment and heard the approaching sirens. She had the theatrically expressive face of a kindergarten teacher, her mouth making an O.

Irene looked up the slope into the untended orchard. The grass between the trees had been mowed but the branches met in tangles overhead and hung low between the rows. "Ask them to bring the ambulance down as far as possible," she said.

Irene had left her car up in the grassy expanse between the tall white farmhouse and the various outbuildings, but she had carried her kit down with her, a case containing the rudimentary tools she'd need to begin the investigation of an unattended death. Quickly now, moving with some urgency, she set to work, knowing that the dispatch had been heard all across the county and that behind the aid car would be patrol deputies and the entire detective contingent from Shelton, a horde of people trampling about in performance of their duties, who would perforce contaminate the scene.

She unzipped the soft-sided case and quickly pulled out the camera and began recording a panorama from where she stood, turning slightly with each frame to capture a full 180 degrees of the orchard on the left, the slough, and then the dune and the path leading to the beach on the right. She photographed her own feet and the stubble surrounding them, then the ground to either side and ahead of her, including a trampled patch where a cigarette butt had been crushed out, which she collected in a ziplock bag.

She took a series zooming in on the body and a telephoto panorama of the far edges of the slough. Who knew, something could show up, some bent reeds or a patch of torn cloth.

She moved then to the right onto a path and entered a dim tunnel leading through a belt of tall firs and cedars choked with an understory of salal, Oregon grape and huckleberry, and in a moment emerged into the brilliance of the beach. It was like a secret passage, like the wardrobe in the children's classics that opened onto an entirely different world. The beach. You knew it was there but still were unprepared for it. The light and the sudden expanse. The heat. Sandy here at the upper reaches, giving way to pebbles, then rocks further down.

The tide was partway out. Or partway in. Irene didn't have the tides firmly fixed in her head, though she should. She knew that they ebbed and flowed with the moon in such a way that there were two highs and two lows roughly every twenty-four hours, but in all the passing of various waterways over the last several days during the normal course of her workday, the schedule of the tides had not registered on her. It would be a help right now to know if the tide was coming in or going out, but it wasn't readily apparent. Unless roiled by wind or wakes, there was no surf in the protected waters of the South Sound and the tide rose and fell imperceptibly. In any event, the sand was dry underfoot so there was no hope of finding meaningful footprints. Dry, so it was probably coming in. Therefore the low had probably been three hours earlier, and the next high would be three hours hence.

Last night when the squall hit the tide would have been high. She would have to check to be certain. She knew the moon was full and that extraordinarily high and low tides accompanied the August full moon. Irene wondered if she had been taught the science behind the tides in school and had failed to retain it. She didn't like having this hole in her knowledge base handicapping her now.

She walked north on the beach along the jumbled driftwood and dune grass until she came to the outlet from the slough. Pickle grass, which was a succulent and not a true grass at all, wove together into a solid blue-green mat along the edges of the channel, and Irene gave up on staying dry and walked in the streambed itself, letting the water flow over her paddock boots. Standing at the lip of the slough, now looking across at a different angle to where the body floated, she shot another panorama. In this series the approaching paramedics would appear, led by Rosalie down the orchard path.

She had done what she could to preserve the scene as she found it. Most likely her photographic documentation would yield nothing but scenery and ordinary landscapes containing no useful information. But Irene was a great believer in the camera, not necessarily as a divining tool but simply for its recording abilities. She would pin the panoramas to her office wall, and in the coming investigation she'd be able to reenter this moment when her mind was still fresh and hadn't yet been dulled with detail, presumption and frustration.

Irene turned and shot the Guevara house, the just-completed mansion to the north, visible now beyond the poplars. People in town who had worked on it called it Chez Guevara—a grandiose shingled and gabled structure rambling across a mown hillside, more hotel than house. She had not seen it before, though she'd heard about it when it was under construction. She wondered what the Paris family thought of their new neighbor to the north.

Looking out across the water, Irene shot a panorama of the Sound from where she stood—McMicken Island far to her left, nearly touching the shore of Gustavus Island, a sort of Pacific Northwest Isle de Saint-Michel where people waded at low tide to pick oysters, then Heron Island further out and larger, and finally the long horizon of the Long Branch Peninsula a mile and a half away across Case Inlet, the destination of the blackberrying flotilla described by Rosalie. Even on this blue midsummer morning, scrubbed clean by last night's storm, there was not a vessel or a sail in sight on these remote waters of the Sound. And hardly any dwellings visible on the forested land masses.

III

ourteen hours later the long northern twilight was fading. The slough and the surrounding beach and orchard were strung with yellow crime tape, electric in the dusk. The body was long gone. The Mason County Sheriff's Department was done for the day.

Irene was the last to leave. It was her case. By rights this was fair, it should be hers, but she knew better than to make the assumption it would be assigned to her. The five detectives in the department were supposed to receive assignments based on workload rather than seniority or anything else, a method that afforded Inspector Gilbert plenty of latitude for interpretation. There were only so many ways to play favorites though, and eventually it could come back to bite you. Irene had been bumped off the vacation roster by the more senior detectives who requested August leave, and now one was fishing in Alaska in the middle of his two weeks and another was scheduled to start his time off in a matter of days. The other two were working with Kitsap County deputies on a narcotics investigation. Irene had just made an arrest in a burglary case and had a possession with intent to sell going to court. Last night she'd been a fifth wheel on the Kitsap collaboration. Inspector Gilbert's hands were tied. By default Irene got the case.

She turned and walked slowly up through the darkening orchard toward where she had left her car. Lights were on in the Paris house. Irene didn't know where it came from, perhaps it was universal, but other people's lit windows always gave her a pang, a forlorn feeling of exclusion. She wondered what was going on in there. She wondered if they were trying to get a meal together despite the circumstances; if Dr. Paris and his remaining two children and their children and spouses and the houseguests and housekeeper were all gathered together in the kitchen of the tall, ramshackle farmhouse perched here on the bluff above this empty northern stretch of beach as they had done each August for thirty years. Irene knew from her own experience the relentless insistence which the mundane imposes on grief. The children are hungry, you have to eat.

She stayed in the shadows and moved closer until she was standing just outside the patch of illumination thrown by the kitchen window. It was as she had imagined, the family gathered there, or some of them, moving about, the children at the table, someone at the sink, the housekeeper tending something on the stove. It was kaleidoscopic, as though choreographed, the passing back and forth, grave and formal like an old-time line dance. Something caught her eye and Irene looked up in time to see movement in a dark upstairs window. Someone watching her watching them through the kitchen window? Who? Whoever it was was in Anne's room, the dead woman's room. She'd been in that room herself earlier in the day, opening drawers, looking in pockets, collecting items.

She was going to get to know them. It was a complicated family, she had learned that much already. Everyone, the neighbors as well, had been interviewed by one or another of the detectives, and tomorrow morning Irene would have everyone's initial statements typed up and on her desk. She'd have the basic information of who everyone was and how they fit in relation to the dead woman, where they were last night and what they said they'd seen or heard. A start, something to build on.

Irene slipped away from the light and went around the house and past the barn. As she got into her car she smelled cigarette smoke. Somewhere not far away in the falling dark, someone was smoking and watching her.

She turned the car and drove up the steep track that tunneled through the woods and out to the dirt road before she turned on her headlights.

⚬

VICTOR WAS at home. Always a relief to her. He was sprawled on the couch watching a boy-and-his-dog DVD he'd rented, a choice that made him seem young and innocent and which made Irene's worries seem pointless and premature. But she knew better. The woods in Mason County were full of trailer houses where people cooked methamphetamines; and in greenhouses and garages lit by grow lights and in atrium windows, cannabis flourished. Sometimes when Irene got home at night hip-hop or rap was blasting from behind Victor's closed door and he emerged only reluctantly and had nothing to say. Sometimes he wasn't home at all. "Hanging out with friends," he'd say when he came in late and she asked where he'd been. "Call," she said, "or leave a note. Otherwise I worry." It was hard to know what limits to set on a fourteen-year-old boy in a small town in summer. Or how to enforce those limits. He had a job bagging groceries and stocking shelves at the corner store and he mowed lawns around the neighborhood as well. He had his own money, time on his hands, and only one parent and she could pay attention only part of the time. Sometimes Irene was worried to distraction.

"Hi, honey," she said.

He pointed the remote and paused the movie. "Hey, Ma." He looked up and she ruffled his hair. Irene Moran and Luis Chavez together had produced a thin, brown-eyed, olive-skinned, dark-blond boy of sublime beauty. His perfection caused Irene to live in perpetual fear. In him she saw Luis. His skin was thin as silk, teeth fragile as glass, bones like twigs. Sometimes she couldn't help herself, when she looked at Victor she saw Luis, battered, broken, a nightmare she couldn't make go away. She kissed Victor's forehead and smelled sweat and gasoline—reassuring, wholesome, hard-working boy-in-summer smells. "I'm going to watch," he said, and started the movie again.

"Okay," she said.

"I made macaroni," he added, "and didn't eat it all."

⋘⃟⋙

Irene stood in the kitchen eating leftover macaroni and cheese out of the pot with a wooden spoon and thought about the dead woman—Anne Paris, Oliver Paris's third child and second daughter—the body across town now in the coroner's office in a refrigerated drawer with a tag on her toe.

Irene didn't yet know with certainty the cause of death, but she knew certain facts about Anne Paris. Twenty-nine-year-old white female, only child of Oliver and Julia, younger half-sister to Leland and Libby, unmarried, a Barnard graduate. She'd attended medical school at the state university and was now—well, had been—a psychiatrist in psychoanalytic training, following in her parents' footsteps, on staff at an elite, privately funded Boston mental institution. Last seen going out alone in her brother's small, fast sailboat, the International 14. She'd been hit hard on the back of the head and had spent some time submerged in cold water. She was wearing a Hawaiian-print bikini top and bicycle shorts when she died. No life preserver.

Irene could feel her mind engage. She was already thinking about tomorrow, formulating a mental list of the order in which she would proceed. This was not always the case. Her work was often discouraging and sometimes boring. The hours were long and the pay was only adequate. The county was depressed, the timber industry hit hard by the economic downturn. County coffers were depleted and budgets cut, the sheriff's department included. Crime was up. Worse, though, was the lack of camaraderie.

There was no overt disharmony among the detectives or within the department in general, but a woman on the force changed the dynamic, of that she was certain. Moreover, she'd come up from Los Angeles after four years with the L.A.P.D. and the Mason County boys were determinedly unimpressed. Irene didn't let it bother her. They could work together, and did. She went out for a beer with one or another of them from time to time to demonstrate she was a good sport. But they weren't really friends and she never felt covered. And that was a difference. L.A. was dangerous and depressing and she'd wanted out almost from the beginning, but there was always somebody watching her back. She was part of something. Here they gave you a car and a gun and if you called for backup it could take half an hour. She'd hired on as a deputy on patrol and she knew better than to think Inspector Gilbert had really wanted her to move up when he had an opening in detectives. But she was the most qualified candidate, and the sheriff was running for reelection and diversity looked good for the department. Plus, no one wanted to risk a disgruntled woman with a grievance dragging through the protracted process of Public Employee Relations Commission hearings.

It was funny how things worked out. She'd grown up here. In this town. In this house. When she left she'd never looked back. Never planned on coming back. She would have laughed if anybody had said she ever would.

The house itself was pleasant enough. A two-bedroom clapboard saltbox built in the twenties on the hill south of town. It was solid and there were some nice details—the ceilings were high, the downstairs floors were hardwood. From the upstairs bedrooms you could see the inlet and the Simpson timber mill. Through parsimony and indifference the house had been spared the usual unfortunate fifties and seventies updates. It was plain and old-fashioned. Irene had pulled up the carpeting, refinished the floors, stripped the wallpaper, and painted the walls white, trying to erase her childhood memories and evidence of her parents.

There were no sidewalks in this part of town and plenty of space between the houses. It seemed a very long way from Los Angeles. Irene had come back for that reason. She couldn't safely raise Victor on a cop's pay in a city where everywhere you looked there was somebody who had everything and having things seemed to matter—cars and clothes and leisure. In Los Angeles if a boy had money he'd stolen it or his parents gave it to him. Gardeners mowed the lawns, not neighborhood boys. Immigrants bagged your groceries and washed your car. There was always someone willing to work for less. You couldn't instill values, or Irene couldn't imagine how you could.

Assigned to gangs, she started busting kids hardly older than Victor, truant teens with guns and drug habits, and it was time to get out. She came home to Shelton and made an uneasy peace with her father and cared for him until he died. Her mother was already gone.

⁂

"Night, Ma," said Victor, standing in the kitchen doorway, "I'm going to bed."

"Give me a kiss," she said. He rolled his eyes but walked over—he was already as tall as she—and presented his cheek for her kiss. This semantic interpretation of her request was understood between them and made her smile. Victor was moving away, detaching. She was bound to lose him, and trying to hold him would only push him out the door.

After he'd gone up, she poured two fingers of Bushmills into a juice glass and added an ice cube. This had become a habit, a way of ensuring sleep. A habit she must monitor.

She realized she'd been standing in the kitchen for a long time, leaning against the counter, lost in her thoughts of tomorrow and of the Parises and her worry over Victor. She walked through the living room and roused their old Australian shepherd from where he was sleeping beside the couch. He got stiffly to his feet and followed her outside. Irene stood in the warm night looking up into the stars while the dog made his bedtime rounds in the yard.

III

"She didn't drown. She did aspirate seawater, but not much. It was the skull fracture that killed her. Did you see it?" Irene had seen it the day before when they first hauled the body out of the slough and performed a preliminary forensic examination—a sickening depression on the back of the head. Now though, Chesterine Reade rolled the body as she spoke, without waiting for an answer. The back of Anne Paris's head had been shaved. Irene's stomach lurched.

"What did it?" Irene asked.

"A stick. A branch. Possibly a pipe of some sort. Something along those lines. Not a rock, in other words, or a hammer or a frying pan. Something more or less cylindrical about three inches in diameter. At least that's what I think. Look." Chesterine had glasses dangling on a chain around her neck which she positioned on the bridge of her nose as she bent forward over the body.

Irene obediently leaned in close.

"See here?" said Chesterine, pointing to aspects of the wound with the tip of a pen. "And here? See the laceration, how the skin is torn? Whatever hit her wasn't completely smooth. Not like a baseball bat for instance. There was a knob or a knot or a protuberance. Some sort of asymmetry."

"The boom of a sailboat?" asked Irene.

"Well, I don't know," said Chesterine. "Are there fittings of some sort? I'd have to see the boom." She rolled the body over again onto its back. "She had sex shortly before she died."

"Does it make sense that if she were hit by the boom and knocked overboard that she was dead by the time she hit the water?" Irene asked. "Not breathing? We know she was sailing."

"Sure. Anything's possible. These water ones are hard. You lose so much evidence. Even time of death. The water's cold and certain processes are retarded and other stuff is just washed away. But we'll know a lot more when we get stuff back from the lab. And Felix will be up this afternoon."

Chesterine was the Mason County coroner, an elected position. She was a licensed practical nurse and a paramedic, qualified to determine cause and manner in most unexpected or unexplained deaths, but not a doctor and not qualified to perform an autopsy. Felix Guzmán, M.D., once the Pierce County Medical Examiner, had left that position in disgrace following a scandal involving photographs, the deceased mayor of Tacoma, and a particularly morbid autopsy assistant. Dr. Guzmán retired to Olympia and in time regained something of his reputation, working as a consultant assisting smaller counties and municipalities as a freelance forensic pathologist. Chesterine, a tall, potato-shaped person with a no-nonsense coiffure, and the imperious, dandified Filipino doctor made peculiar allies, but they liked each other and their combined expertise was formidable.

"Look at this, though," Chesterine said. She lifted an arm and swung it away from the body so Irene could see short blue stripes on the pale inside of the upper arm. "Same over here," pulling the other arm away from the trunk to reveal similar bruises. Chesterine replaced the arms and leaned across the table and took hold of Irene's arms, not hard, but hard enough to suggest how such markings could come to be made. It was an imploring gesture, a grasp simple to break free of. "That's just theory, you understand," said Chesterine, dropping her hands. She picked up a clipboard and began reading. "Five foot eight, 130 pounds. No apparent surgeries. Oval mole inside right thigh, two centimeters. Eyes blue, hair blonde, chemically highlighted. All her own teeth. No wisdom teeth. Pierced ears, pearl studs. Small compass rose tattoo mid-back at L-4. Paint flakes and sand under the finger-nails, no apparent blood or tissue—we'll do more testing on that. Semen in the vaginal swab."

Irene looked down at what had been Anne Paris. A long, slender trunk—one of those long-waisted girls men love—smallish, wide-apart breasts, narrow waist, flat stomach between prominent hipbones, long thighs and shapely calves, delicate ankles, toe-nails painted an iridescent car-body maroon. A Matisse sort of figure. It was hard to tell if she had been beautiful. Not pretty certainly in a conventional way, but unusual and perhaps oddly compelling. Full lips. Imposing narrow nose. Surprising dark eye-brows. She looked dead but from the front, undamaged.

"Has the family been in?" Irene asked. "The father?"

"No," said Chesterine, "not necessary in these circumstances. You know, identified at the scene."

"Oh. Right."

Irene picked up Anne's hand and held it in her own. A big hand for a girl, bigger than Irene's, narrow with long fingers ending in almond nails and manicured cuticles. Irene's own hand was dark against the pallor of death, broad across the knuckles, bony and strong with pale, rounded nails. Irene still wore her wedding ring, a narrow gold band. She'd never taken it off, not once, in all the years since Luis put it there. She was superstitious about that. She put Anne's hand down. Chesterine was looking at her. There were ways that you tried to breathe life back into somebody, get into their skin, know them when all possibility of knowing was past. You had to, in a way, to do the job.

Mason County didn't own a morgue. Instead the county rented space on an as-needed basis from the local funeral home, keeping bodies in the prep room cooler. One of the other drawers was occupied. "Who's that?" Irene asked, changing gears.

"No one you know. John Doe suicide, Soundview Motel. Wrists. Checked in as Jean D'Eau, if you can believe that," giving it an exaggerated French accent. "The cops have it." Which explained why Irene hadn't heard about it. The town cops had jurisdiction within Shelton city limits, it wouldn't be a matter for the sheriff's department.

⋘◈⋙

IRENE WAS glad to be able to get in the car and drive. The morgue rattled her. She wanted a shower or a barbiturate or a drink. None of them possible or advisable at this moment. She wished now she hadn't touched Anne's hand. It gave her the creeps. There was a period of time, she thought, when the spirit had left the body but hadn't gone far. Maybe roosting up in the corner of the room or hovering somewhere close-by. She felt observed and obliged now, beyond just the job.

Luis she had touched as though he could feel pain—was *in* pain—gently gathering him to her as if her caress might heal him. But then she had shaken him and tried to call him back. It had seemed as though he wouldn't have to go. He hadn't been gone so long that he couldn't turn around. Clinging to him, to the dead but not yet cold, corporeal, battered part of Luis, she watched the rest of him walking away down a hall and she screamed his name, "Luis!" But he didn't hear or wouldn't turn around. "Luis! Luis!" Half lying on him, clinging. The officer in that case standing back with averted eyes.

She couldn't allow herself to think this way.

IV

ustavus was an island about twelve miles long and three
miles wide, tapering to points at each end, roughly two-
thirds the size of Manhattan and similar in shape. About two
hundred people lived on the island, more in the summers. During
the forties and fifties, families from Shelton and Olympia had
bought bits of beachfront property and thrown up cabins built
on pilings over the sand or perched on the bluffs above. The
interior of the island was still largely owned by timber companies, Simpson and Manke, huge tracts of second growth fir and
cedar ending in cliffs high above the beach, precipitous drops
impractical or impossible to negotiate, which made much of the
waterfront undesirable as vacation property. Thus, long stretches
of beachfront remained uninhabited.

The beach itself sloped gradually, leaving wide expanses of
sand exposed at low tide. In the sixties a bridge replaced a six-car
ferry, making access to the island less suspenseful, but even so
the population grew slowly.

Thirty-five years earlier Oliver Paris and his newly acquired
second wife had purchased an old farmhouse and orchard in
order to have something to do with the children during August
when shrinks famously took a month's vacation and Oliver had
three weeks' summer custody of the children of his first marriage.
The property was located on Fergus Point, a broad promontory
midway along the east side of the island with wide sandy beaches
and a view of Mount Rainier.

In those days, a research facility attached to a now-defunct pulp mill attracted scientists to Shelton, and a cultured stratum of PhDs bifurcated the scrappy mill town. Among these was Fritz Strauss, a British chemist who had been a childhood friend of Julia Sachs in London, both children of Austrian Jews who had fled Vienna in the late thirties and made their way to England. Fritz left London for the U.S. and graduate school and never returned. When Julia Sachs was offered a fellowship at the Menninger Clinic in Topeka, Kansas in the mid-sixties, they reconnected and remained in touch. Later, Fritz and his wife Janet had two boys similar in age to Julia Sachs Paris's brand new stepchildren, and a cabin on Fergus Point. In this way the families began a tradition of summers together, which continued now into a third generation.

THE PARIS property consisted of a couple of cottages, a scatter of small outbuildings and a two-story barn, as well as the house itself, all painted a powdery white, flaking now to the wood beneath, surrounding an expanse of bleached mown grass, forming a compound of sorts where an older Honda minivan with California plates, a vintage Mercedes, and a Dodge Neon were randomly parked.

Irene rolled to a stop and got out. It was still early, not yet ten, but already hot. The buildings had reached that stage of decrepitude where they seemed one with the landscape, camouflaged and natural. Oddly, the shabbiness of the estate conveyed a gentility that Irene found at once appealing and intimidating, a total disregard for convention that bespoke privilege.

A thin fringe of tall yellow grass missed by the mower skirted the buildings. Moss grew on the roof shakes. Next to the house a pale pink rose climbed a trellis to the porch roof where a faded green whirligig in the shape of a roadrunner spun its wings when the breeze caught it. Foxgloves and an espaliered pear tree grew against the end of the barn. At the edge of the bluff a collection of weathered Adirondack chairs faced the Sound. Somewhere unseen in the orchard someone was running a mower. In an upstairs window a corner of a lace curtain lifted, then fell back into place.

Irene caught her reflection in the cottage window and swung her jacket to cover the gun under her arm. She wore plainclothes, black jeans and a gray tee shirt, a uniform she put on every day; but as a matter of decorum she didn't like to display her hardware and she always wore a jacket, even in summer.

Softly, a call from behind her, "Good morning, Detective Chavez."

Irene turned. Ira Logan was standing in the open barn door. How long had he been watching her? Eyes everywhere, making her jumpy. Ira was the dead woman's boyfriend. She took a breath. "Morning," she said, and walked over. Behind him, up on blocks in the dim interior of the barn, was a 1963 TR3, his summer project—this much she'd learned the day before—rewiring it and creating a solid walnut instrument panel.

"I didn't mean to startle you," he said.

"You didn't," she replied and immediately regretted it. His look clearly announced his skepticism. He was a young doctor, trained to observe. Now she was flustered. She walked past him into the barn. The floor was packed dirt soaked with decades of spilled motor oil. As her eyes adjusted she could see a jumble of tools and lumber filling the other side of the barn, an overturned rowboat resting on sawhorses, garbage cans, and evidence of past summers in the form of a child's deflated wading pool, badminton racquets and a croquet set. Various sizes of faded orange Mae West life vests hung from the rafters. A rusted barbecue. And interestingly, against the back wall, a rumpled down sleeping bag spread on a canvas cot under a trouble light dangling from an extension cord.

"So," she said, turning back to the Triumph, "this is it?"

"Yes."

She glanced at him, smiling. "It's so small. It's teeny."

"You're like six inches off the road," he said. "Makes a Miata seem huge. You have no idea."

"How's it going," she asked, looking at a tangle of colored wire spilling out from under the dash.

"This?" he asked, and rubbed his face. He was tired, she could see, or anxious, or both, a muscle jumping at the corner of one eye. "Well," he said, taking a breath. "It's going well. It's not complicated, you know. It's quite straightforward and much simpler if you're doing it all at once. I have a manual and it's like connect the dots. The only hard part is that the space is tight and often you're working blind. You know, you can't see your hands and your hands are too big."

She looked at his hands, big competent hands with grease-blackened fingers like Victor's. Not like a doctor's scrubbed hands at all.

"But wiring is simple," he went on, "positive, negative, ground. It's not mysterious, your choices are very limited." There was a pause. "How's it going for you?" he asked. "Have you learned anything?"

"It's early days," said Irene. She was glad to note that he said "like" like a kid, it made him more ordinary. She had to remind herself not to be too impressed by these people. Most of the time as a cop or a deputy sheriff you dealt with lowlifes, the sad edges of society, and it was going to be a challenge to probe and inquire into the genteel, educated, opaque Paris family. "What did Anne think of this project?" she asked.

"She wasn't in the slightest bit interested," Ira said. He looked away, squinting, and Irene thought his eyes might have filled with tears he was trying to hide.

"You know, I taught her how to drive a stick shift," he said. "Up here actually, on the island, years ago now. We've been together seven years," turning to look at her, "did you know that?"

"Really?" said Irene. "That's a long time."

After a moment he went on. "She'd never driven a stick before but she had this thing about cars, or at least she conveyed that she had a thing about cars, like we shared an enthusiasm, you know, and she wanted me to teach her."

He looked at Irene and pursed his lips, stopping himself, she thought, from going on. Then, in a different tone, "Anne is a very accomplished flirt—was—and she flirted with me over cars once upon a time. But when it came to this Triumph, she wasn't in the slightest bit interested. She was studying for the psychiatric boards and I was working on my car. If you want to know the truth, we weren't even sleeping together. She wanted to stay up late reading and studying. I wanted to fall into bed at ten o'clock. I've been sleeping in here. Or in the orchard sometimes to catch a breeze." A silence. "Someone was going to tell you."

Ah, thought Irene, he had noticed that she had noticed the cot. "Explain to me about the psychiatric boards," she said.

"Oh, it's not that big a deal, it's a test, that's all. Not everybody is good at tests. Anne certainly isn't. This was her third try. She was embarrassed and she'd had an ultimatum from Atkins, where she was practicing. You know, pass the boards or you can't see patients kind of thing. But everybody knows medicine is like the Ivy League in a way, you're not going to flunk out. They'll hold your hand. She got through medical school, she did her residency—she's a good doctor, I know that. But you do have to sooner or later pass these board exams. Anne—she's been tutored, she's done everything. She's just not a test taker. It's a hoop you've got to jump through and most people jump through and that's it. Everybody knows you're a doctor, it's a formality. But it was eluding her, it was an embarrassment. She was taking them in Seattle this time and she was determined to pass. It was a monkey on her back. I mean, jeez, she was what, three years out of med school." He sighed, then said bleakly, "But it was making her a bear to live with."

Irene looked at him. Ira had faintly Mediterranean good looks—a tumble of dark hair, fair skin, quite a lot of moles, and one of those sprouts of beard beneath the lower lip.

"It hasn't soaked in." he said. "I'm glad to have something to do," indicating the car. Then, in another tone, regaining himself, "What happens now?"

"Now," she said, "I'm going to talk to everybody. Starting with Dr. Paris."

"Again?"

"Again," she said. "There's a lot of talking in my business too."

"Shrinks listen, remember? And answer questions with questions. They don't talk." He smiled, his gloom lifting. "Will you be coming back to talk to me?"

Irene laughed—as she was meant to—at his deliberately plaintive tone. "Oh, yes," she said.

"Well," he said, smiling now, "till then, then."

Ira Logan, Irene thought as she walked toward the house, was quite an accomplished flirt himself, making an interview with an officer of the law seem something like a date.

Chesterine had said that Anne had had sex. With whom, Irene wondered.

⚜

AN ELONGATED lean-to of a back porch containing a bathroom and a woodshed had been tacked onto the side of the kitchen at some point in history to replace the outhouse, which still tilted out in the orchard under a mantle of climbing wild rose. Irene heard water running behind the closed door. Someone was showering. She peered through the screen into the kitchen, which seemed to be empty. There were dirty dishes piled on the counter beside the sink under the window. "Hello?" she called, and waited. There was no response. "Hello?" Nothing.

She stepped off the porch and walked to the edge of the bluff, which was alarmingly close to the house, and looked over. The cliff face was slightly concave here, undercut beneath where she stood. An old cedar growing nearby dangled roots into thin air. Below on the beach a mound of sandy earth gave evidence of a slide. Each year, Irene imagined, the precipice moved a little nearer. Soon you'd get vertigo standing at the kitchen sink.

Behind her she heard the bathroom door open and she turned and saw Nikki Roth, the other Paris houseguest, Anne's best friend, step naked out onto the porch, toweling her mane of hair. She tossed her head, flinging her hair up out of her face and back onto her shoulders, scattering beads of water, and saw Irene watching. She laughed and wrapped herself in the towel, but not hurriedly and not before Irene had gotten an eyeful of her extraordinary cloud of pubic hair, pale gold on either side of a dark brown center stripe. Nikki was deeply and evenly tanned, apparently *her* summer project, and naked she wore a pale bikini of milky skin.

"Oops," Nikki said, securing her towel. "We're quite uninhibited around here."

"I'm looking for Dr. Paris," said Irene.

"Oh, well, he's in his study," Nikki said, as though stating the obvious.

"Which is where?" asked Irene.

"I'm sorry," said Nikki, instantly contrite. "I didn't mean to be unhelpful. It's just that if you know him you know that that's what he does. He gets up, he drinks his coffee, he goes to his study. Every single day."

"Even today?" asked Irene.

"Even today," said Nikki. "Or especially today. It's the little white cottage on the other side of the house near the pump house. The little one. Do you know where I mean?"

"I can figure it out," said Irene.

"We're not quite ourselves," said Nikki, "I'm sure you understand."

Well, thought Irene, as she walked on around the house, having circled it now and come back to where she'd parked, she wasn't sure she understood at all. Uninhibited indeed.

❦

Dr. Paris's study was a one-room cottage, open to the rafters, everything painted white. It looked, Irene thought, very much like what she imagined a shrink's office would look like, except more rustic. There was a table piled with books and papers, and what seemed to be a single bed slipcovered in ivory linen, a threadbare Oriental carpet, his leather chair and ottoman, and the pressed-back kitchen-style chair he offered her, in which she now sat.

Dr. Paris was quite tall and very thin, he had enormous feet which he now rested on the ottoman, making a teepee of his knees. He was gangly and loose like a marionette, which, along with the oversized feet, made him seem youthful, though otherwise he appeared frail. He wore corduroy pants and a gray suit coat buttoned over a dark blue cashmere muffler that was folded across his chest. Quite bundled up despite the heat. They sat in silence.

Irene looked out the paned window above the table at her car parked in the open area between the buildings. Sitting here he would have seen her arrive. He would have seen her use his window as a mirror. His dusty window like one-way glass. He would have watched her go into the barn with Ira and then come out again and walk around toward the back of the house.

She waited. He had an unusual tolerance for silence.

"Dr. Paris," she said finally, and stopped. She looked around the room. On top of a high, narrow dresser, a chipped porcelain pitcher held a bouquet of wild sweet peas. He followed her gaze.

"She picked those," he said. "Anne." He spoke slowly and softly and Irene could hear a hint of a Southern accent.

Irene didn't know what to say. There was another silence. She shifted in her chair.

Dr. Paris put his feet on the floor and leaned forward to square a pile of loose pages covered with angular handwriting lying on the table. He cleared his throat. "You know, Detective Chavez," he said, "this is very difficult. I'm an old man. I'm very tired. To you it may seem pertinent how my daughter died, why she died, when she died, at whose hand or by what means. To me what's pertinent is only . . ." He trailed off. He took a shaky breath and looked out the window. "If there is something you must ask me, ask me. Otherwise, please go."

"Dr. Paris," said Irene—then, "Excuse me, sir." Her phone was vibrating. She stood to take the call. "Chavez," she said, and walked outside.

It was the Coast Guard. They'd found the boat, the I-14. It was beached a mile or so south. If she wished, seeing as she was there on the island anyway, they'd have the officer zip up and collect her and she could take a look for herself.

⚜

IRENE GOT what she needed from the car, the camera and evidence bag, then walked down through the orchard toward the beach without saying anything more to Dr. Paris. She'd try again on another occasion. He'd be relieved, that was all, watching her go, leaving him alone in his study with his grief and his writing and with the flowers picked for him by his now-dead daughter. She could feel his eyes on her back as she walked away.

V

A boater had called it in, the Coast Guard officer told her. Someone passing on the water who had seen the I-14 lying on its side high up on a deserted stretch of beach.

A lapstrake hull, narrow and deeply V'd, of painted boards with an improbably tall mast, the International was famously fast and notoriously unstable. It wasn't a class of boat intended for casual sailors. It was a fourteen-foot racing sloop, a little day sailer with a retractable center board rather than a fixed keel, no cabin or instruments, just an open cockpit with cleats and pulleys to manage the sheets, designed to be single-handed.

The tiller was broken, the long handle that attached to the rudder, splintered off at the transom. In a big wind and high seas, the Coast Guard officer said, a panicky sailor might try to hold an impossible course, hauling on the tiller until the wood snapped.

Irene looked out at the Sound and tried to imagine these placid waters as they must have been two nights ago, gray and turbulent and perilous. This morning in Case Inlet there was not a breath of wind to fill a sail.

Some distance from shore a seal broke the surface as Irene watched, and looked around, a head like a periscope. It saw her and studied her for a moment, then sank below the surface again. The beach here was rockier than at Fergus Point, and more steeply pitched. A curve of the shore created something of a cove, a wide shallow bay at the base of a nearly vertical cliff rising several hundred feet above a tangle of willow and alders.

Irene took photos, examined the boom and the gunwales and took scrapings in case some tissue might turn up. But the boat had capsized and it seemed unlikely that salt water wouldn't have washed away all trace of anything that would be of interest.

There was sand and seawater and a sodden half-full pack of Camel Lights inside the boat; and when Irene was finished she helped the officer tip out the water, then they pulled up the center board and righted the vessel and furled the sails. Irene sealed the soggy cigarettes in a plastic evidence bag. Then together they hauled the I-14 down the beach to the water's edge and set it afloat again, fastened to the launch on a long line. The Coast Guard officer would tow it to Shelton for further forensic examination.

Irene declined a lift back to Fergus Point. She wanted to walk back along the beach. If she hurried she could beat the tide. In the worst case she'd get her feet wet, and she was already soaked to the knees from wading out to clamber aboard the Coast Guard launch.

She didn't think it was very professional, and Inspector Gilbert might not approve, but there was no one to see and a long way to walk, so she took off the paddock boots she habitually wore, tied them together by the laces and slung them over her shoulder, and set off barefoot. The sand was warm underfoot and the sun hot on her shoulders. She stopped and took off her jacket and tied it around her waist. It was, she thought, a small stolen moment of summer vacation and she wished she could share it with Victor. In this northern climate you could live near water and forget to take your kid to the beach. In California, they'd often gone out to Santa Monica, or further north to Point Dume or to small coves along the Pacific Coast Highway, to picnic and swim. Here in Puget Sound the water was very cold and only the stalwart swam. If the weather held, Irene thought, maybe they'd go out to the coast on her next day off and hike to the shore at Cape Alava.

Her thoughts wandered, not really focused on anything, idly observing her surroundings, the sand and pebbles underfoot, shore birds, the vegetation growing on the bank. The incoming tide. So it was with a jolt that she suddenly registered the completely unexpected presence of a figure on the beach some distance ahead of her.

She didn't know how long it had been there or if it had just now appeared. At this distance she couldn't tell if it was moving toward her or away or moving at all. And she couldn't tell if whoever it was was aware yet of her presence. She moved closer to the leaning frieze of trees so anyone looking in her direction wouldn't see her as a silhouette against the sand, but would have to make her out through a scrim of branches. Here she stopped and put her jacket back on, then retrieved her field glasses from her bag.

When she located the figure through the lenses and brought it into focus she had another shock. The figure, which was a man, now magnified to intimate proximity, stood facing her with his own set of binoculars trained upon her, seemingly close enough to touch. It was weirdly unsettling. No normal behavior suggested itself, a wave or salute. Irene noted a description before dropping her glasses. Dark hair, trim graying beard, slender. Dark blue tee shirt tucked into khaki pants. Impossible to determine height or anything else about his appearance with the binoculars held to his face. She guessed he had gotten a good look at her, however. She wondered if he'd seen the gun.

She began walking toward him, continuing to watch with her naked eyes, curious to see what he'd do—disappear, await her, approach her?

And he vanished. He was there and then he was gone. He simply faded into the trees and vanished while she was still quite some distance away. She tried to keep the exact spot fixed in mind as she approached, but when she came up to where she believed he had stood she was no longer certain. The pebbly sand didn't hold a footprint.

She wished she'd thought to flash her badge. Fish her wallet out of her back pocket and flip it open next to her face for his watching binoculars. Perhaps then he would have waited. She had no way of assessing whether his disappearing act was in itself suspicious. There was nothing official about her appearance to compel him to wait or to reassure him if he had seen her gun. He might have been alarmed or simply not have felt sociable. Perhaps emerging from the trees and imagining himself alone and finding he was not, he simply chose to retreat.

Irene stood still for a moment, perplexed. Then she put down her boots and her satchel, ducked through the branches and found herself in a grotto-like space formed between the bank and the overhanging limbs of alder and cedar. It was cool and dim, and Irene could see that although the bluff had appeared uninterrupted, here it was cut by a narrow canyon under a canopy of towering trees. The walls of the canyon were covered with moss and maidenhair fern and glistened with seeping water. A foot or two above the beach the suggestion of a path led steeply uphill from a bank of tangled roots. In the damp sand at the base of the bank Irene saw the hoof prints of a deer and what looked like a track made by a tire tread, which she recognized as having been made by a Mexican huarache.

Somewhere up in that ravine, hidden in foliage, a man was watching her. She would like to talk to him. She'd like to know who he was and how he came to be on this particular stretch of uninhabited beach, and what he might know about the I-14 and its occupant during the storm that had dashed it ashore.

She pushed back out to where she'd left her shoes, and looked north along the shore trying to gauge how soon the incoming tide would make the beach impassable. It was impossible for her to tell. She had a tide table in her satchel and the times of the tides now fixed in her head, but that information alone wasn't enough to determine at what point the water would be up under the trees and spars, blocking her passage.

The seal was back, keeping tabs on her. It snorted. A sort of wet woof. Irene sat down and brushed the sand off her feet and put her boots back on.

It was cool and damp after the heat of the beach. And quiet, like stepping into a room deadened by carpet and drapery. She climbed silently upward on a footing of moss and duff. Somewhere in the trees above a woodpecker hammered intermittently. The canyon widened as she ascended, and flattened into a glade. There, door handle-deep in nettles, was the husk of a car dating from some time prior to the late fifties when Irene's mental catalogue of makes and models began. At some point then this path would have been an actual road, or enough of a road for an auto to negotiate. Unless perhaps, and perhaps more likely, the car, no longer working, had been dumped, pushed over the lip of the canyon and had landed on its wheels.

Further on the undergrowth became thicker and clogged the way. Here a track angled in from the north to join the canyon, unused and overgrown but once a road of sorts. Irene had to step over fallen tree limbs, but the going was easier, and before long she emerged at the top onto level ground. Here the track she'd been following became more defined, two negotiable ruts wending away into a forest of second growth timber, a plantation of closely spaced Douglas fir, naked trunks shooting straight up over a hundred feet, interspersed with alders, and towering above a dense understory of elderberry and hazelnut. Sunlight filtered through the canopy.

Now that she was here, Irene had no idea what she had imagined to accomplish with this foray. There was no sign of the fugitive from the beach. It had been a waste of time and worse, imprudent. He could be anywhere. He could have been watching the entire adventure. She felt like "it" in hide-and-seek. She imagined herself cupping her hands to her mouth and hollering "olly-olly-oxen-free" to make him emerge.

It was lighter to her right toward the bluff and Irene walked in that direction, hoping to get a glimpse of the beach in order to assess the progress of the tide before retracing her steps. And there, as she shouldered through a huckleberry thicket, she came upon a mossy cabin in a clearing.

She approached cautiously. A padlock fastened the door, suggesting there was no one inside. She knocked anyway and waited. There was no response. She circled around, found a window, and looked in through cobwebs. It appeared to be a single room with a sleeping loft, crudely built, studs and rafters exposed, plywood floors. There was an incongruous stuffed armchair from some earlier epoch upholstered in faded pink velvet, and an enameled wood-fired cookstove. In the loft, a mattress on the floor, and suggesting more recent tenancy, one of those ubiquitous black rollaboards and a stack of books and papers beside the chair. She could see a cheap Styrofoam cooler next to the stove and a thirty-five millimeter camera with a long lens on a table. Beyond that, not much else. Irene wished she could make a closer inspection.

Aside from the obvious signs of a current resident, the cabin appeared abandoned, unused for decades. A blackberry runner climbed up the inside of the window she was looking through. And outside the forest was encroaching. Alder saplings grew right up against the walls, and foxglove and fireweed pushed up between the boards of what was left of a stoop. Irene wondered whose land she was standing on. She had supposed that the entire tract here above the beach belonged to Manke, but perhaps she was mistaken.

Irene continued toward the bluff, pushing through the alders and thigh-high yellow tansy until she could see the water. A slide at some point had taken a chunk of the bank and a lounge chair perched crazily partway down. Trees had been knocked over and leaned every which way like jackstraws, obscuring her view of the beach.

She turned back toward the cabin and found something of a path leading inland, which she followed until she came to a junction where the grass was trampled and there was a turnaround pattern of tire tracks. She had not heard an engine, but she supposed that there had been a car parked here and that her quarry had decamped. She felt more comfortable, no longer imagining herself watched.

Irene wondered where the track would come out if she followed it. Here it seemed to run north, parallel to the beach. She had a pretty good mental map of the island, and it seemed likely that after a walk in the woods she'd emerge on the county road within a mile or less of Fergus Point. Alternatively, she could return to the beach and hope she could still get by. She felt truant at this moment, no longer confident in her judgment. It seemed unprofessional to be alone in the woods. No one knew where she was. She thought about calling in to the office but couldn't pick up a signal on her cell phone. That was often a problem in Mason County, pockets where you'd break up and go dead.

VI

"I'm not sad, I wouldn't say," said Libby Paris, now Burton, Anne's older half-sister. "Or not yet. It hasn't soaked in. I just feel weird and rattled. It's like things seem normal, and then you remember. I mean, we're all always quite scattered here, and then we congregate and scatter again. Everyone's always doing their own thing. It's like at any moment she's going to come walking around the corner of the house."

It was Libby who Irene had heard mowing earlier in the orchard. Libby was taller than her dead sister and narrowly built. Hips like a boy. A blue bandana was knotted over her hair. She was flushed beneath her tan and wore a coating of sweat and chaff so that she looked slightly blurred, as though seen through gauze or Vaseline.

"Mowing seemed like a good idea," she said. "At least it was something to do that was actually useful."

꧁꧂

IRENE HAD emerged from the woods about where she'd expected, and had continued along the road and then down the narrow track of the Paris driveway. As she'd passed the study she imagined Dr. Paris watching her, puzzling over her reappearance from this direction. She had walked on around the house and found Libby splayed in an Adirondack chair drinking a bottle of beer.

"Hey," said Libby, looking up.

"Mrs. Burton," said Irene, "hello." She was relieved at the prospect of restarting her day, conducting the business she had planned.

"Libby."

"If you prefer," said Irene.

"I do," said Libby.

She had offered Irene a beer, which Irene would have liked but declined, and water, which Irene accepted and which Libby produced in a half-quart Mason jar with ice and lemon. Now they sat together in the chairs in the sun. Across Case Inlet, in the sky above Long Branch, Mount Rainier loomed.

"Was she killed?" asked Libby after a moment. "Do you know that for a fact?"

"It's a suspicious death, Mrs. Burton."

"Libby."

"When we have the pathologist's report we'll know more."

"But you think she was killed."

Irene didn't answer.

"When we lived in New York, years ago after Elliot and I were first married, the man upstairs, Evan Rhodes—funny, I still remember his name—his wife was murdered. It freaked us out. It seemed dangerous or unlucky to know him. But sophisticated too in a weird way. You don't think about that happening to people you know," she said, "people in your own circle. Murdered."

After a while, when Irene didn't say anything Libby asked, "Do you think that everyone always thinks, why can't we just make it yesterday? Just rewind the tiniest bit? Because the world seems the same in every respect except that one. I mean, the sun is out and it's pleasant. Soon it'll be time for a swim. How are you supposed to hold onto that one bit of information which changes everything? I can absolutely picture Anne walking around the corner of the house right this minute and flopping down in a chair, and she'll say something and you'll instantly forget about me." Libby sighed. "She was very charismatic." They sat in silence.

"You don't smoke do you?" asked Libby after a while.

"No, not anymore." Irene answered.

"Neither do I," said Libby, "or at least I don't buy them anymore."

"Did Anne smoke?" asked Irene after a moment, thinking of the cigarette pack in the I-14.

"No. Not officially. Unofficially she smoked. She used to hand me her cigarette if she was smoking and Oliver appeared. Or Julia, when she was alive. Sometimes I'd be sitting there holding two cigarettes, mine and hers." She laughed. "It was comic. I mean, they're shrinks, they're smart, but even so, they only see what they want to see. Selective inattention, they call it in the trade. In some ways Anne never grew up."

"Oliver. You mean Dr. Paris?"

"Yes."

"And Julia. Anne's mother?"

"Yes. She died last year very unexpectedly. A brain aneurysm." She was quiet for a moment. "It's astonishing how much you can miss someone you never really liked."

"You didn't like your stepmother?"

"No, not particularly."

"But you miss her now she's gone."

Libby was silent for a long time, then said, "I miss the way things were. I'm going to miss Anne."

"Have you always called him Oliver?" Irene asked, "your father?"

"Yes," said Libby.

"Somewhere I read that very bright children will do that," said Irene.

"Oh, that wasn't our case," said Libby quickly. "It was him. His idea. Some mid-twentieth-century egalitarian notion or something. Erase the patriarchal hierarchy. When Anne came along though, she called him Daddy." Libby's face crumpled momentarily and she looked away, fighting back tears.

Irene wondered why, what it was in that thought that stabbed her. And then she was composed again.

"So, how *did* you get along with your sister?" Irene asked.

"Is this where I say I'd like my lawyer present?"

Irene couldn't help it, she liked Libby. "If you want a lawyer it's your prerogative. I'm just collecting information."

"I got along fine with Anne. We never had words. Not once." She turned and looked directly at Irene. "That's the truth," she said.

At that moment Libby's two boys skidded around the corner of the house on bicycles, armed to the teeth—BB rifles slung across their shoulders, cap guns in their belts. They let their bikes drop by the porch and approached shyly, looking at Irene.

"Hi, Mom," said Owen, the older one, who was ten as Irene recalled. Neal, the younger brother, leaned against his mother's chair.

"Hi, boys," said Libby. "Where've you been?"

"Playing with Sam and Jared," said Neal.

"Are you hungry?" she asked.

"Yes," said Neal.

"Are you the deputy?" Owen asked Irene.

"I am," said Irene.

"Detective Chavez," said Libby.

"I'm Owen," said Owen.

"I know," said Irene, "I've been briefed."

"Do you have a gun?" he asked.

"Yes."

He thought this over. "Can I see it?"

Irene flipped her jacket open and he craned to look. "Are you left-handed?" he asked.

"What makes you ask that?" asked Irene.

"I don't know. It's on your other side. I just wondered."

"Well," she said, "you're right, I am left-handed." She smiled at him. "Are you?" And he nodded, packing his own pistol on his left hip.

They were cute kids, she thought, thin and tan and very blond and quaintly boyish, playing outdoors with old-fashioned ordnance and bicycles instead of inside with electronics. She felt a wave of envy for Libby, and a yearning for Victor as he'd been at ten.

It was now mid-afternoon, and one by one the Paris family and their guests appeared around the corner of the house and assembled in the chairs by the bank.

"Stay for lunch," they said. "You must."

Someone brought out a bottle of chilled white wine. Someone flung a yellow cloth over the picnic table. A breeze came up and stirred the branches high in the fir trees, ruffling the water out on the Sound.

Irene felt like Alice down the rabbit hole, not at all in charge of events.

⁂

IRENE'S OWN interviews the day before gave her a sketch of the family, along with the interviews conducted by the other officers and detectives, the notes of which she'd glanced at that morning, now so long ago.

Leland and Libby were children of Oliver Paris's first marriage which ended when Libby was seven and Leland nine. Libby had moved back to Texas with her mother, a schoolteacher, now dead, while Leland stayed with his father and new stepmother in San Francisco. Thus the brother and sister grew up in different worlds with little shared experience.

Anne was born two years following the divorce.

Libby became a satellite child—her words—every other Christmas and three weeks each summer, until as a rebellious teenager she put a stop to the visits altogether. As an adult she had remained remote from her father and his family until the death of her mother when loyalty no longer constrained her and she had children of her own, and she began spending August on the island once again.

Leland and Libby both married young. Rosalie was Leland's third wife and together they had a three-year-old daughter, Phoebe. From his first marriage Leland had teenage boys whose whereabouts were unknown, swallowed up along with their mother into Scientology and never heard from. Leland was a genetics professor at UC Davis and Rosalie stayed at home and looked after Phoebe.

Libby and her husband Elliot, an actor, who had been off the island for an audition and who had returned in the small hours, lived in L.A. in the Hollywood Hills. Libby was a photographer— sometimes friends hired her for weddings or to take portraits of their children, and sometimes they hired her for housecleaning. During the school year she worked as a substitute teacher. Money was tight.

And the houseguests, Nikki Roth and Ira Logan, Anne's friend and boyfriend respectively since undergraduate days. Nikki was completing a residency in gynecology at Mount Auburn in Boston, and Ira was an emergency room physician just back from three months in Ecuador where he'd been part of a measles inoculation program organized by Doctors Without Borders.

Also in residence was Yvonne, the French housekeeper brought along from San Francisco, who, despite forty years in the United States—almost all of it in the employ of Julia Sachs—was still unable to communicate in English. Julia had spoken French, and so had Anne, but Dr. Paris did not, and he and Yvonne managed with a common vocabulary consisting largely of culinary nouns. Dr. Paris knew enough to request fish for dinner—*poisson*—or to convey that a guest was expected—*compagnie*—and beyond that there was no directing Yvonne's behavior anyway.

⁂

THEY BROUGHT out cheese, and cold salmon under a mesh dome, tomatoes swimming in balsamic vinegar, a plate of figs wrapped in prosciutto, and a long loaf of homemade bread that Yvonne brought to the table in a flood of tears and French. "Anne made it," explained Rosalie, sotto voce. "It's the last of the bread that Anne baked."

Everyone looked at Dr. Paris, who simply took the serrated knife and the breadboard from Yvonne and sliced the loaf without the slightest change of expression. He sat in a straight-backed chair at the end of the table. He had turned up the collar of his suit coat, though the sun was blazing, and added a hat, a stained gray fedora. The place to his left on the bench was unoccupied, unset. Anne's usual place, Irene surmised.

Libby went inside to make grilled cheese sandwiches for her boys and for Phoebe, which made Irene feel slightly more normal. To her, lunch, if she ate it at all, was fast food or a container of yogurt.

It was silent around the picnic table. Only the clink of cutlery and the drone of circling yellow jackets, attracted by the salmon. Irene wondered if meals were always like this or if the silence was because of Anne. Their faces gave nothing away.

Then Dr. Paris looked up and froze, his attention focused north toward the slough. Irene turned to follow his gaze and saw a figure approaching up the orchard path. It was a burly middle-aged man wearing a Panama hat, holding a German shepherd dog on a short leash and carrying a bottle in his other hand. The sun went momentarily behind a cloud. Dr. Paris rose and the man stopped about twenty feet from the table. Everyone was still. It was like a tableau vivant illustrating some ominous moment out of Chekhov.

"Dr. Paris," the man said.

"Mr. Guevara," said Dr. Paris.

"Forgive the intrusion. I've brought a 1982 Latour à Pomerol which I hope you'll accept with my condolences," said Mr. Guevara. It was a little like watching a tennis match, the two principals spaced far apart and all heads swiveling from one to the other.

"Thank you," Dr. Paris said finally. "That's very kind." Some inarticulate cue passed between him and Leland, for Leland climbed out of his place at the picnic table and walked toward Mr. Guevara. The German shepherd growled, arresting Leland's approach.

"Phsssst, Gus." said Mr. Guevara, silencing the dog. And then to Leland, "I am so sorry." And he leaned down and stood the bottle carefully upright on the uneven turf.

Suddenly Phoebe screamed. Everyone looked. A yellow jacket on the back of her hand. Rosalie slapped it away.

"Baking soda," said Libby. "Quick."

"Meat tenderizer if you've got it," said Ira.

"Ice," said Owen.

"Make sure the stinger's out," said Nikki.

"Yellow jackets don't lose their stingers," said Leland from where he stood, seizing a pedagogic moment while his daughter yelled. "That's only honeybees, and it's fatal—they die—but yellow jackets can sting again and again."

Rosalie jumped up, scooping up Phoebe, and hurried into the kitchen.

"Can I have the rest of her sandwich?" asked Neal.

"No," said Libby. "She may still want it."

Calm settled back over the scene, though inside Phoebe was still crying and Yvonne was exclaiming, *"Mon Dieu! Mon pauvre cherie!"*

Mr. Guevara touched his hat, then turned and departed.

Leland walked over and picked up the bottle and delivered it to his father. Dr. Paris sat back down and put on glasses to inspect the label. "How extraordinary," he said.

Leland climbed back into his place at the table and looked at Irene. "There's been a dispute," he said. "Mr. Guevara has built steps from his property down onto ours and he's been walking across our dune and using our beach. It's very aggressive and annoying. Have you ever heard of the right of adverse possession?"

Irene had not.

"I have the same wine," said Dr. Paris. "In 1982 I bought twelve cases of this same wine when it was still in the barrels in Bordeaux. The weather that year in Bordeaux was magnificent. It was hot and dry. It was an exceptional year. I did a lot of research and made a very sound investment. This is not an easy wine to come by. It's now much sought after. I have always considered this *my* wine. How extraordinary," he said again.

"What will you do now about Mr. Guevara?" asked Libby.

"There's nothing to do," replied her father.

"Don't you think it's a peace offering?"

"If Mr. Guevara wants peace with me all he has to do is remove his steps."

"Well, it's a gesture."

"It's a gesture with no meaning," said her father.

Inside the phone rang. Dr. Paris got up and went into the bathroom on the porch.

Irene tried her cell phone but again couldn't get a signal. She got up from the table and walked around the house, trying again beside her car, but there were still no bars. The phone had worked from here earlier in the day. Dr. Paris walked past, returning to his study. He didn't see her or feigned not seeing her. She went back to the table.

"It's more than just topography," said Leland when Irene mentioned her telephone difficulties. "Wind, humidity, particulates in the air. Sometimes you'll get a clear signal and other times nothing. Aircraft. Your batteries, many factors affect the signal."

Rosalie emerged from the house with Phoebe on her hip, a big plaster of baking soda across the back of her hand.

"Is that the first time you ever got stung?" asked Owen.

Phoebe nodded, two fingers in her mouth.

"I've been stung hundreds of times," said Owen.

"Owen," said Libby.

"Well, I have," he argued. "Lots, anyway."

"We shouldn't eat outside," Rosalie said peevishly. "At this time of year the orchard is full of wasps. It's dangerous to walk there."

"I don't know that that's true," said Leland.

"Who called?" asked Elliot.

"Oh," said Rosalie. "It was for Anne. I didn't know what to say."

"Who was it?" asked Ira.

"It was your landlord, calling from Boston. He told me his name but I've forgotten already."

"Julian?"

"Julian."

"I could have taken it," said Ira.

"I didn't think of that," said Rosalie. "Phoebe was crying and it just seemed so weird and I couldn't think what to say. I just said she couldn't come to the phone at the moment."

VII

hile Irene was on the landline inside trying to explain to the clerk in the county assessor's office which plat maps she wanted copied and on her desk by the close of business, lunch around the picnic table had devolved into a general removal to the beach. Irene came out of the house to find the table cleared and everybody gone, except Ira. He dangled an aquamarine swimming suit by one strap. "Here," he said, "Everyone's gone to the beach."

Irene was nonplused.

"Or not," he said smoothly. "It's up to you. We always swim in the afternoons. Or some of us swim and the rest sit on the beach."

"I'm working, Dr. Logan."

"Sure. Whatever," he said. Then quizzically, "You can't ask questions in a bathing suit?"

"Whose is it?" asked Irene.

He hesitated. "Well, yes, there's that."

How extraordinary, Irene thought, what a bizarre proposal. She wondered if Ira cared at all that Anne was dead, or if her death hadn't registered yet, or maybe it was a callous veneer intended to mask his true feelings. Or maybe he thought he was merely being hospitable, thinking of her as a guest to be included in the afternoon's activities, put at ease in awkward circumstances. She couldn't tell. Whatever it was, it was bizarre.

"I'll walk down with you though," she said, "I want to look at the steps. Mr. Guevara's steps."

"You'll be hot," he said, looking her over.

"Oh, well," said Irene. Ira was wearing loose trunks and a grease-stained tee shirt and Teva sandals, she noticed. He stood up and slung a towel over his shoulder and together they set off down the orchard path.

"Why are you interested in Mr. Guevara's steps?" asked Ira.

"I'm interested in everything," said Irene. "Why do you suppose your landlord was calling?"

"Oh, I know why he was calling," said Ira.

"Why?"

"We're late with the rent. Anne didn't want to write the check."

"Why not?"

"Why do you think?" he asked.

Irene didn't answer, waiting.

"You know, I don't know why," he snapped, looking away. "She probably thought it was my turn. She was quite meticulous about pecuniary matters. But I'm just back, you have to realize, from three months of unpaid humanitarian work and I'm a little strapped."

"So what was going to happen?"

"What do you mean?" he asked.

"Well," said Irene, "I mean, it wasn't going to go away, right? The rent."

"Anne got help from her family," he said. "She had it, I didn't, it's that simple. This month I didn't have it."

"So she was going to pay?"

"Eventually, yeah."

Irene could tell he was annoyed. He didn't like being pressed.

"Were you guys splitting up?" she asked.

"I don't know," he said. "But it wasn't going well." He paused, as though considering what to say next or whether to say anything.

Irene waited.

"She had a beef, you know." He shot her a look. "I wasn't a hundred percent straight arrow in Ecuador and she knew it."

"How'd she know that?" asked Irene.

"She just did," he said, subject closed.

"How?" Irene persisted.

"If you must know," he said, "I brought something back." He flashed her a look.

"As in?" Irene asked.

"As in an STD."

"Ah," said Irene. "I see."

"It was nothing," he went on. "It meant nothing and she knew it was nothing. It was stupid and meaningless. But obviously I had to tell her. We had to be treated, both of us."

"How'd she take it?" asked Irene.

"You know, like anyone would. Who was it, what was she like. How could I, why did I, how many times, was she pretty, did I love her. Maybe it was that or maybe she was preoccupied, but she just quit talking. I don't know if you've noticed yet, but this family, they can be perfectly pleasant and at the same time as remote as Pluto. It's like a door closes. I mean, she was completely opaque. I've been with her for seven years but I had absolutely no idea what was going through her head. She could have decided something about us and I'd be the last to know."

"What will you do now?" Irene asked.

"About what?"

"About the rent."

"I don't know," he said. Then after a moment, "That's a good question. I hadn't thought about it. But I can't imagine going back there to live."

"All your things are there," said Irene, "and hers."

"Books and clothes," Ira said, "everything else is hers."

"It's an apartment?"

"Yeah," he said, "actually the third floor of a house. He lives in the downstairs. Julian, the landlord."

"In Boston?" Irene asked.

"Cambridge. Same thing, just across the river."

Irene was quiet, thinking. "Dr. Logan," she said, "perhaps I'd better speak with your landlord."

"You're kidding," said Ira.

"I'm not kidding," said Irene.

They walked in silence for a few moments. "I just want to finish my car and get out of here," Ira said morosely.

"Well," said Irene, "you mustn't do that without first speaking to me."

<hr />

Irene could see where the offending steps had been, but they were gone. Removed or washed away by the tide. Mr. Guevara's clipped green lawn rolled down toward the beach and ended abruptly at a chest-high seawall of poured concrete. Where it ended—just at the edge of the outlet from the slough where the wild beachfront belonging to the Paris family met the groomed Guevara property—the earth was washed away.

"They were built of log rounds," said Leland. "Varying lengths stood on end and sunk into the ground to make a little staircase." Leland waded across the channel and crouched down, scraping at the sand with the side of his hand. "Here," he said, "look." Irene crossed to join him, soaking her boots once again. There in the sand he had uncovered a tarnished brass monument set into a stone, placed long ago by the United States Geological Survey. "Here's the property line," said Leland. "You can see how his steps came down onto our land and he's worn a path across our dune."

She looked over her shoulder where he pointed at the bruised and trodden sea grass and pickle weed.

"The right of adverse possession," he went on, "is this arcane law that says essentially that if someone uses someone else's property for some certain period of time under certain specific circumstances, eventually they can legally claim it as theirs. Most people have never heard of such a thing, but Mr. Guevara is a lawyer."

Irene looked up toward Mr. Guevara's house. Little pink streamers of tape fluttered at intervals along the edge of the slough. She wondered if they'd been there yesterday and she'd failed to notice. She couldn't remember. "Someone's done a survey," she said.

Leland straightened up and looked. He was tall like his father, though unlike him thickening through the middle. He wore a bristly mustache and clip-on sunglasses over wire-rimmed bifocals. "Whaddya know," he said.

"Was that tape there yesterday?" asked Irene.

"I don't know," he answered, "I couldn't say."

"It doesn't matter," said Irene. "It's easy to find out. I took photos."

⁓⁓⁓

IRENE AND Leland turned and walked back towards where they'd left the others on the dune. It was hot, but in the angled northern light the fringe of trees behind the beach reached cool fingers of shadow across the sand. Here, even at summer's zenith, you were reminded of evening or the approach of fall—some coming chill.

It looked like a normal summer afternoon, towels spread on the sand and a red-and-white umbrella casting an oval of shade over Phoebe. The Strauss brothers, Nigel and Peter from down the beach, along with their wives and children, had joined the group, their canoes pulled up onto the sand. But the adults were silent and somber in the sun, not reading or talking, while the children played at the water's edge. To Irene it looked like something out of a magazine illustrating how other people lived, the completely unselfconscious languor. Or someone's memory of a perfect summer, the image that captured an earlier time of innocence or happiness or childhood. Looking back there'd be no way of knowing which afternoon of which summer—everyone so young. How old were the children? What year was it I wore that bathing suit? Or you'd look for Anne. Was it before or after the summer Anne died?

"Who's going in?" asked Leland as they approached, producing a kind of general shift in the languorous scene and a clamor from the kids, "I am! I am! We're already in!" they shouted.

Irene watched as everybody got up from their towels, stepped out of shorts, peeled off tee shirts, then moved down to the water's edge where they waded in and stood at various depths hooting and exclaiming at the cold. Ira plunged in and began a crawl straight out as though he meant to swim across to Mount Rainier.

Nikki and Libby stayed on the dune, reclining against a driftwood log. "I'm having a medical consultation," Libby said to Irene.

"That's fine," said Irene, "I'm on my way. I'm done here for the day." But she continued to stand for a moment watching the swimmers and thinking of her growing to-do list. Ira was right, she was overdressed and hot.

Nikki's exuberant pubic hair escaped the edges of her bikini in a blonde nimbus, and as Irene watched she sprayed a mist from a plastic bottle across her thighs and stomach. Ah, peroxide, Irene thought. That explained that. One mystery solved.

Nikki saw Irene watching and laughed. "I tried waxing one year and it was *excruciating*," she said.

Irene smiled. The effect, Irene thought, was oddly celebratory and more comic than provocative, like clown's hair.

Libby's boys were calling for her to come in. Irene knew that she should move on, out of earshot of whatever it was Libby was relating to Nikki, back to her own world and neglected responsibilities; but she stayed where she was, standing behind the log the other women leaned against, oddly languorous herself, mesmerized by the brilliance of the afternoon, the sparkle off the water dazzling her.

"You need to be treated," said Nikki.

"Treated how?" asked Libby.

"Flagyl. It's quick and effective but unpleasant because you can't drink any alcohol while you're on it."

"A calamity," said Libby and laughed. "And then that's that? It goes away?"

"It does," said Nikki.

"Hallelujah. Will you write me a prescription?"

"I will," said Nikki. "It'll be out of state but usually no one cares."

"Can I swim? I mean, is there any reason not to?"

"Swimming's fine," said Nikki.

"Well, then," said Libby, and she got up.

Flagyl. It was ringing a bell. An empty vial in the drawer of Anne's nightstand that Irene had collected yesterday, along with birth control pills and a bottle of Xanax.

"What does she have?" asked Irene as Libby walked away. She wasn't sure that Nikki was going to answer.

"Giardia," said Nikki finally, looking up at Irene.

"What's that?"

"It's a bug, a protozoa. Gets in your gut."

"Did Anne have it too?" Surprising Nikki.

"Uh-huh," she replied. "Yes, she did. She was over it now. They have to test the water. There's something in the well. A mouse fell in and drowned, or a mountain beaver. No one's drinking the water."

Pellegrino on the table at lunch.

Nikki got to her feet. "Now I'm going to swim before they all come in."

Far out, Ira had turned and was swimming back toward shore. Rosalie stood in the shallows swinging Phoebe. Libby's boys and Sam Strauss were wrestling over an air mattress while their mothers swam parallel to shore, doing the sidestroke, their heads out of water. Nikki ran down the beach and splashed in up to her knees, made a shallow dive and came up whooping.

Irene turned and walked along the dune to the path. She wished there were a way she might have put on Anne's aquamarine suit and become a part of them for the afternoon.

⌘

NEAR THE house Irene encountered Dr. Paris, who appeared agitated.

"Detective Chavez," he said, "come with me a moment." He led her to the end of the barn where there was a stoop and a door that opened into an old granary—now a tool room—running the width of the barn, floored with wide planks and partitioned off from the rest of the building. At the back of the room a flight of stairs disappeared upward. A workbench occupied the wall beneath a cobweb-dimmed window and under this was a wooden packing crate placed on its side containing dusty bottles of wine. Dr. Paris lowered himself onto one knee and Irene crouched beside him.

"Every year I bring up a little wine when we come," he said. "Something nice for special occasions—you cannot find a decent bottle of wine in Mason County—and over the years a bit of a cellar has accumulated out here in the barn. There's no inventory and I don't remember from one year to the next what I've brought up or how much has been drunk. However, I was certain there was a bottle of the '82 Latour à Pomerol. And there isn't." He pulled one dusty bottle after another out far enough for Irene to see the labels. "'82," he said. "That's a very old and very valuable wine."

He looked at her. She could see the direction his mind was working. He levered himself up, a hand braced against his thigh. Irene stood beside him.

"You don't think it's possible, do you," he asked, "that he's been in here and now he's given me a bottle of my own wine as a peace offering?"

Irene didn't know what to say. She didn't know whether it was more plausible that the dignified old psychoanalyst was entertaining an elaborately paranoid fantasy or that Mr. Guevara indeed was so baroquely Machiavellian. "I don't know how you'll ever know the answer to that," she said finally.

"No," he said. "You're right, of course. But now I must mistrust either my memory or my neighbor."

"Or anyone else," said Irene. "It isn't locked, is it?"

"What?" he asked.

"The barn."

"Oh, no," he said, "not when we're here. We never lock anything. When we're gone, of course, in the winter, we lock up."

"So anyone could have come in here and taken a bottle of wine."

"Why?" he said.

"Well, to drink, I suppose," said Irene. "I don't know."

"Without permission?"

Irene shrugged. "Maybe."

Dr. Paris just looked at her. He was attached, she could see, to his own scenario, intent on believing that his mind was playing tricks or his neighbor was. "Where do the stairs lead?" asked Irene.

"There's a loft where Libby and her family stay."

"May I look?"

"Unfortunately, Detective Chavez, apparently you are entitled to do anything you choose. You may look, if that is what you want. I'm going back to work."

Irene went up the stairs and looked into a long, low unfinished room extending the length of the barn up under the eaves. There were mattresses on the floor and a chest of drawers, books and board games, clothes hung from the rafters, and a fan backed up against a small window. It was very hot. Irene looked but didn't linger.

VIII

The western sun blinked through the trees as Irene drove off the island, dazzling her. She called home when she could pick up a signal, but the machine answered and she didn't leave a message. In the car she felt more herself, in her own world with the radio crackling. The Paris family, she realized, rattled her, left her upset and feeling inadequate. She would be a part of their world until she knew how Anne had died, coming and going and inserting herself, but she was an alien on Fergus Point, a visitor from another culture. She must remember this.

Irene had gone to high school in Shelton with the Strauss boys, the Parises' friends from down the beach. Nigel was in her class and Peter one year behind. There was one occasion at the end of her senior year, skip day they called it, when nearly the entire senior class cut school and drove out to Gustavus Island. They swam and sat on the porch of the Strausses' cabin drinking beer and talking about the past and future, and for one afternoon—too late for it to matter—they blurred the distinctions that stratify small-town high schools. When the sun went down they built a bonfire on the beach and roasted marshmallows, and Nigel Strauss, the research chemist's son, draped his arm around Irene's shoulder. At that moment anything seemed possible—any pairing, any future.

After that they went back to class and reassembled into their cliques and groups, took their finals and went off to college or to the army or to June weddings and small-town jobs. But for Irene that one day opened a window.

Irene's father had worked his entire life in the woods as a logger until he couldn't any longer because of age and injuries, and then he worked in the mill. Her mother was a retail clerk at J. C. Penney's until the store closed, and then she worked as a home health aide until she couldn't do the lifting. Irene hadn't thought about college. At eighteen she hadn't thought about much of anything. But two weeks after graduation she packed a few things into a secondhand VW Rabbit, and she and her best friend Cherry left Shelton behind. They headed south to build new lives for themselves. Outside of Stockton the water pump on the Rabbit gave out. They took a room at a cheap motel, and when their money ran out they got jobs with housekeeping and tried to save. After a couple of weeks Cherry gave up and caught a northbound Greyhound for home. Irene moved into an apartment that a Mexican girl she worked with shared with her brother and two other girls.

In the fall Irene enrolled in community college, quit the motel and went to work picking walnuts. She liked being outdoors in the pale fall afternoons. Without intending it her life became entwined with the farm workers, with her roommates and their families, illegal aliens who came north to work in the fields. She went to workshops and organizing meetings. She tutored her friends in English and the Pledge of Allegiance. Lives outside of her own engaged her. It took her four years, but she got her AA degree and was accepted at UCLA. By then she had met Luis Chavez.

Irene hadn't planned on Luis. She had her life mapped out. She was determined and self-sufficient. She'd get her bachelor's, then a JD and a career, perhaps specializing in immigration law. She spoke Spanish, though she couldn't write it. She tried to resist Luis. Over and over she told him it was over.

Luis was legal. He'd crossed at Brownsville when he was sixteen and during one of the amnesty windows he'd gotten his citizenship. He was a carpenter, his English was nearly unaccented, and he was culturally assimilated. He drove a blue Ford pickup and played the harmonica. Kids loved him. He had mournful eyes, teeth white as soap, dusty brown skin. He was tall and thin with rounded shoulders and wristbones like doorknobs. His palms were warm and hard as cement. Irene couldn't resist him when he smiled. He liked his work and didn't yearn for anything he didn't have, except Irene. In the evenings he'd come around to the house she shared and sit on the stoop drinking a beer, fixing things that were broken.

When Irene told Luis she was going to Los Angeles, he said he'd go with her. She said no and he drove away and didn't come back. A week later she was washing dishes and watching out the kitchen window when he pulled up in front of the house after work and swung down from his pickup. He was wearing dusty jeans and steel-toed work boots with logger heels, and a faded tee shirt with the sleeves ripped out. He bounded up the walk and when she met him at the door he took her hand in both of his and dropped to one knee. In his pocket he had a plain gold band with *Luis & Irene* engraved on the inside.

They were married in Stockton by a justice of the peace in front of a few friends.

In Los Angeles they rented a stucco bungalow in Culver City beneath the landing pattern of LAX. Luis found work and made a decent wage, and Irene went to school in Westwood and worked part time in the registrar's office. It wasn't a bad life. They made friends and cooked sometimes in the backyard. They went dancing on Saturday nights when a band played in the tavern down the street, whirling on the ends of each other's arms or all wrapped up together and barely moving. They went to the beach and sometimes to the mountains or out to the desert to hike in Joshua Tree. Once Luis took her to Monterrey, Mexico, to meet his mother before she died.

Irene was twenty-four and pregnant when she graduated from college. Law school would have to wait. They moved to Van Nuys and Irene stayed home with the baby until he was three. When he started preschool she got part-time work answering the phones in a law office. In time she took a prep course and scored high on her LSAT; and when Victor began kindergarten in the fall, Irene was going to be starting her first year of law school at UCLA.

You thought life would go one way, one day following another, and you looked ahead and imagined you could see the way things would be tomorrow and the day after, and on into next year and beyond.

Luis was jumped in a bank parking lot only blocks from home one evening when he stopped at an ATM to deposit his paycheck. He gave his attackers his PIN code but they beat him anyway. Or maybe they beat the number out of him. It didn't matter. They used rocks and fists and feet.

An arrest was never made.

Somewhere along the line during that first summer after Luis died, Irene had made an adjustment to necessity. She had a child and was now his sole support. Grief was a luxury and she couldn't afford it. Irene closed a door. Now she couldn't go to law school—that was out. Three years of tuition and no income, and student loans to pay back at the end of it. But a receptionist's pay wasn't adequate.

Some of her friends thought vengeance motivated her to join the police force, but it wasn't that—the training was quick and the pay was good. She just wanted a job, some way for a single mother to provide a reasonable life. She requested a graveyard shift and got it because no one else wanted it, and she hired the daughter of someone Luis had worked with to sleep over at night. She was home in the evening to make supper and to give Victor a bath, and to read to him before bed. And home again in the morning before school.

Irene was smart and thorough and balanced. She never used her service weapon. Her performance evaluations were uniformly excellent. Her partners liked working with her. She was neat and punctual, her reports were terse and accurate, her penmanship legible. She promised herself never to use crude language, and kept her word. She said sir and young man when other officers said motherfucker.

⚓

IRENE CAME into town along the rail siding—where rolling stock loaded with logs was waiting for an engine—made a right at Lumbermen's Building Supply, and drove up the hill past the Dairy Queen to the gray stone courthouse.

It was a grand building for a small mill town, set high above the street atop massive granite steps. It gave Irene a lift, she had to admit, an ongoing sense of awe and importance to work here. The town cops had a low, modern structure on the other side of the tracks, a typical DMV kind of institutional shoebox of a building with industrial carpeting and no headroom. Here the marble paving in the foyer had been replaced with black-and-white linoleum squares and metal detectors awkwardly embraced doorways like post-modern arbors, but there remained nevertheless an august remnant of reverence for due process. Like everywhere, considerations of space, security and modernization conflicted with the geometry of design, but it was a glorious old building with enough frosted glass, carved wood and soaring marble columns to remind officialdom and citizenry alike of the sober business of law and governance.

The sheriff's offices themselves were a warren of cubicles on the first floor, partitioned by modular dividers that didn't reach the ceiling. Only Inspector Gilbert had an actual door to close.

The Gustavus Island plat maps Irene had asked for were on her desk. She tried calling home again but the machine was still answering.

⚓

IT WAS late by the time she got home, past eight but still light. Victor wasn't there. She opened a beer and carried the bottle out into the warm evening and sat on the back porch steps. For the second time that day she wished she had a cigarette. Most of the time she forgot she'd ever smoked. Above the horizon Venus hung in a pale green sky. The dog brought her a Frisbee and Irene threw it for him from where she sat until he wouldn't give it back anymore.

Seeing Nigel Strauss during the afternoon had upset her. He hadn't recognized her. She supposed he hadn't really looked up and paid any attention. They were all absorbed in their grief and loss in their own ways and she was an intruder, an official, nothing to them and practically invisible on the beach in the afternoon when they all went swimming for the first time without Anne. But seeing Nigel caused Irene to remember the weight of his arm across her shoulders all those years ago, and the kiss that followed. And that made her think of Luis. A breeze was stirring the hot evening air against her skin. She couldn't let herself think in that direction.

She turned her mind back to Anne Paris.

⚜

Julian Bernstein, the Cambridge landlord, hadn't answered when Irene had called, and so she'd left her name and her office, home, and cell phone numbers on his voice mail without explaining why she was calling. He still wasn't at home when Officer Sean Egan of the Cambridge police drove out to the house on Huron at Irene's request and put a seal on the third floor apartment—though by then in Boston it was close to eleven.

Irene wondered what she'd do about Victor if she had to fly east for a few days. She wondered if he was old enough to leave at home alone. What did other parents do, single parents with no family and jobs that took them out of town?

Irene felt like the tar baby, stuck in so many places. For reasons she couldn't account for, reasons beyond the smooth, regular boom of the I-14, Irene was quite certain Anne's death was not accidental. But she wasn't at all sure how long Inspector Gilbert would allow her to conduct an inquiry into a death that the sheriff's department could probably quite reasonably determine to have been an unfortunate boating accident and close the book on. She would have to move quickly to establish sufficient motive, opportunity and plausibility to keep an investigation alive. Tomorrow she hoped to have the autopsy report from Dr. Guzmán, which could—if she were lucky—contain compelling evidence to suggest foul play, though what that would be Irene didn't know. In the meantime she had a search warrant for the cabin in the woods.

IX

I rene glanced at the clock when the phone woke her. It was ten minutes past midnight. The voice on the other end was Harley Rose, one of the town cops, pleasantly informing her that he'd pulled over a couple of kids in a pickup who didn't look old enough to be driving. He'd taken them in and booked them after discovering wrapping papers and a Velvet tin half full of marijuana in the glove box. One of the boys was Victor and she could come pick him up if she wanted.

Irene hung up and pulled on a pair of jeans. Her heart was thudding. This was the moment she'd been dreading, her worst fears realized. Victor in trouble. She brushed her teeth, hoping Officer Rose wouldn't smell the nightcap she'd had still on her breath. She imagined the kind of parent she'd appear to be, slumbering while her stoned fourteen-year-old was out joyriding.

The police station was just down the hill and Irene was there within fifteen minutes, but Harley Rose was in no hurry to get through his paperwork and hand Victor over. Normally peers of a sort, Irene thought he was amused by the situation in which she found herself—an ordinary citizen like anyone else up against the obdurate law.

"That was fast," he said. "The other kid's spending the night."

"Who is the other kid?" asked Irene.

"Patrick McGrath. And he's in more trouble than your kid is."

"How's that?" asked Irene.

"He was driving," said Harley, and Irene felt a small wave of relief. "They say," Harley went on, putting an ironic emphasis on *say*, "that your kid's got a curfew and needed to get home and the McGrath kid's dad was asleep—that part I believe, passed out is more like it—and so they took his keys and helped themselves to the truck."

There was a concession in Harley's narrative that the putative curfew suggested at least some parental oversight, despite the fact that his arch look informed her that he knew that she, like Mr. McGrath, had been sleeping.

"I can take Patrick home," she said.

"Doesn't work that way," said Harley.

"Why not?" asked Irene. She knew as well as he did that there was some latitude there.

"Just doesn't." said Harley. "Release 'em to the parent, and in this case the parent doesn't have a vehicle at his disposal. Can't get into town." Harley smirked and Irene wanted to hit him.

"What about the mom?" said Irene.

"I'm not touching that one," said Harley. "It's a custody deal. He's supposed to be with his dad at the moment."

Irene knew Patrick McGrath. He was a nice kid, a little hyper maybe, but lately he'd been taking Ritalin and seemed more modulated. And Irene knew Patrick's mother, the receptionist at her dentist's office, but she didn't know the dad. He was living in a trailer somewhere out of town and Victor wasn't supposed to go there. Victor wasn't supposed to go anyplace where Irene didn't know the parents.

Victor didn't look up to meet her eyes when Harley led him out. He was silent and rubbing his wrists as he got into the car beside her. They made their way through town, then headed north on Highway 3. Irene was afraid to say anything because she didn't know what would come out of her mouth. Just out of town at the wide spot in the road next to the siding she'd passed earlier, Victor said, "Mom, can you stop? I've got to pee." Hardly more than a whisper. She slowed and pulled into the cutout and stopped. It took him a long time and when he got back his cheeks were wet.

"What?" she said.

"Nothing," he replied.

But Irene knew what it was. Victor had said he needed to pee and Officer Rose had kept him cuffed in the holding cell hoping he'd wet his pants. Petty bullying, safe and seemingly inconsequential, but brutal in its way. Relief had made Victor cry.

Irene turned off the engine and they sat silently in the darkness. She wanted to cry herself, overwhelmed by fury and sorrow. She wished she could gather Victor up in her arms and make it all go away. But she couldn't and shouldn't try, she knew that.

After a while he said softly, "Mom, let's go."

She had called Patrick's father and said she'd come out and pick him up and take him back to town. He could collect his truck and do whatever he wanted about his son.

Irene didn't even know how to begin with Victor, but it was easier to talk in the dark while she was driving and didn't have to look at him. "What were you thinking?" she said finally.

"I don't know," he said.

"What are we going to do?" she asked.

"I don't know," he said again. After a while he added, "It wasn't our marijuana. We didn't even know it was there."

Irene believed him. The knot inside her chest loosened. "But you knew what it was, right? When you saw it?"

"I knew what it was," he agreed. "A lot of people smoke it."

"Like who?" she asked, thinking of all the homes he'd been in, after school and on weekends, the friends and parents of friends. But she knew he was right. Sometimes walking the dog in the evenings she'd smell it in the neighborhood, somebody sitting on a porch or a stoop taking a hit. Most of the time, as law enforcement she didn't pay much attention. You could probably find a stash in the nightstand drawer in a lot of perfectly respectable bedrooms. It was useful though, if you wanted to bring someone in for something else. But it could make people stupid if they smoked too much. Make them soft and vague, sap ambition, blur focus.

Of course Victor knew what it was. Of course he'd been exposed to it, tried it if he wanted to, used it if he liked it. How could she have imagined otherwise? Middle school, the most treacherous years, were behind him and he was starting high school in a matter of weeks. As a parent, sometimes you had to turn a blind eye because if you didn't you'd never let them out of the house. You just had to hope their mistakes weren't lethal.

"Patrick's a good driver, Mom."

"I'm not even going to have that conversation," she said. Small-town kids learned to drive young, like country kids. She herself had let Victor drive from time to time on logging roads or on someone's long driveway. She didn't doubt that Patrick McGrath probably knew how to drive, but there were two issues here, one was driving, the skills required, and the other was the lunacy of thinking they could get away with it. The law took a generalist's view and made no allowance for individual talent or particular circumstances.

Victor told her where to turn.

Mr. McGrath's trailer and its surroundings were dismaying. A single-wide set up on cinder blocks in a clearing in the woods beside a chain-link dog run, a woodpile and a burn barrel. The dogs were going crazy at their approach and there was no need to honk or knock. Victor got out to move to the backseat, and as Mr. McGrath came out of the trailer in the glare of the head-lights, he ducked his head and pointed a finger pistol-fashion in Victor's direction in a way that said, catch you later, kid. Irene didn't like it.

She smelled beer when he got in beside her. "Evening, sir," she said. "Irene Chavez. I'm Victor's mother."

He didn't see her proffered hand or affected not to. "I know who you are," he said, making it an insult.

Nobody said anything on the way back to town. McGrath nodded curtly when Irene dropped him at the police station. Officer Rose would get him to his truck.

"Don't go out there again," said Irene.

"No," said Victor. "I know."

<hr />

BY THE time they got home it was nearly two. In the hall by the stairs before he went up, Victor finally looked at her. She had nothing to say and just made a small, helpless shrug, but tears were starting, filling her eyes. Victor stepped forward then and put his arms awkwardly around her and squeezed hard. "I'm sorry, Ma," he said. "It'll be all right." Of all things, standing there with her boy's arms around her, she felt comforted by a man. His transgression, minor as it was, had catapulted him into an adult world.

<hr />

THE ALARM was going to ring in just over four hours. Sleep, often elusive, now welcomed her and she sank into it like water. Tomorrow she would think more clearly.

X

The phone awakened Irene for a second time shortly before five. Julian Bernstein, Anne Paris's Cambridge landlord, had picked up his messages. He was traveling, he said, vacationing on the Cape, and he had no idea where Mason County was, who Detective Irene Chavez was, or why she was calling him.

"Where are you?" he asked. "I can tell I woke you up."

"You did," she said. "Three six oh. It's Washington State. It's not quite five here."

"I apologize," he said. "But I had no idea and it sounded urgent—you left three numbers. Your office—the sheriff's department, did I hear that right?"

"Right," she said.

"There was a recording. I guess that makes sense now. And the cell number wasn't picking up.

"No need to apologize," said Irene, trying to collect her thoughts. He hadn't noticed that the area code was the same as the Parises', which he had called the day before. She felt quite fuzzy, yesterday's urgency to reach him now a dim memory. "Mr. Bernstein—"

He interrupted. "It's doctor."

Jeez Louise, Irene thought, another one. "What kind of doctor are *you*?" she asked.

"PhD organic chemistry," he replied.

"Oh," she said. "Not a medical doctor then."

"No," he said. "Academic."

"Dr. Bernstein," she said, "there's been a death—"

"Oh, my God," he interrupted.

"I'm sorry to alarm you," she said. "It isn't anyone close to you. But it's a tenant, I believe, someone who rents space in your building." There was silence on the line. "Are you there?" Irene asked. He was processing, she thought, connecting the dots, the area code now registering.

"I'm here," he said. "The connection's not that good. I'm on a cell phone. Who's died?"

"It's Anne Paris, sir," said Irene. "We don't know all the circumstances yet but I wanted to let you know that, for the moment, I've had her apartment sealed." There was a pause.

"What do you mean?"

"Just that someone from the Cambridge Police Department has been out to your house to put a seal on the apartment. It's just a precaution, routine in these circumstances on the off chance that we need to delve further. But there's a seal so you mustn't enter. No one can enter."

"I'm not even there," he said.

"Right," said Irene, "I know. I'm just notifying you. This is just for the moment while we determine cause of death."

"What are you saying?" he asked. "What's happened? Why are you involved?"

"There was trauma to the head, sir, and no one with her at the time, and in this county we investigate all unattended deaths. It's routine."

"I thought you meant an auto accident," he said finally.

"No," said Irene, "not auto."

"What then?" he asked.

"We're investigating," she said.

There was a silence on the other end. When he spoke again his voice broke. "Well, you're wrong about one thing—she *was* someone close to me. I mean, not close but she was more than just a tenant. I was very fond of her and this is extremely upsetting."

"I'm sure it is," said Irene.

"You don't know Anne," he said.

"No," she agreed.

"I need to know more about this," he said. "I need more information. You haven't told me anything. When did this happen? Where?"

"Our investigation is ongoing, sir, and we're not releasing details at the moment."

"Plus," he said, now sounding piqued and out of sorts, "there's income loss, you know. Or could be, if the apartment is off-limits."

"Of course," Irene said. The rent, she thought, the unpaid rent. Now he might never collect it. "I understand. If we need to take a look in the apartment, sir, we'll decide quickly. No one wants this to drag on."

Irene made a note of Dr. Bernstein's cell phone number and hung up. She felt a tiny relief at having one small thing ticked off her to-do list before the day started. But the day *was* started, she realized, and with only three hours of sleep behind her it was going to be a doozy. She could function, she knew that—despite sleep deprivation she wouldn't nod off behind the wheel or with her cheek in her hand while talking on the phone—but she wouldn't function well.

She padded down the hall to the bathroom and watched herself in the mirror as she brushed her teeth. A slender woman in a tank top with a pair of her long-dead husband's boxers riding her hipbones. A brown-eyed blonde with fine, straw-colored hair just barely long enough to pull back and catch into a rubber band. This morning there were purple smudges under her eyes and crow's-feet she didn't remember. To Luis, she had been beautiful. She wondered if he'd find her changed. It had been eleven years. What, she wondered, would he have to say to Victor about last night.

By the time she'd showered and had a first cup of coffee, Irene was feeling improved. For the moment she'd decided there was nothing she could do about Victor. Showering, she had imagined Luis's voice saying it wasn't a calamity, Victor was still Victor, still a good boy growing up in a treacherous world.

The wheels of justice would turn. The charges against Victor and Patrick could have been a municipal court matter, but the amount of marijuana and the borrowed truck made it a felony in the thinking of Harley Rose, and he was, in his words, 'sending it up the hill.'

There was a new county prosecutor whom Irene hadn't yet met and he would pursue the charge or he wouldn't, she couldn't predict; and if he did there would be time enough to decide then what to do. In the meantime, Victor would be cautious and subdued, disinclined to press his luck with his mother or other authorities. Less was probably more when it came to her reaction to the fix he found himself in. Sanctions and recriminations would only turn his remorse to excuses and defiance.

<hr/>

Irene left the house before six, getting a jump on the day, leaving Victor still sleeping. It was already hot. This time of year it was hard to remember the pervasive bone-penetrating damp and chill that was the hallmark of the local climate. On these hot August nights you threw off the bedclothes and longed for a fan to stir the air, and in the morning when you went out for the paper the walk was warm and dry under your bare feet. The northern sun was focused by the atmosphere, intense and immediate.

XI

Irene swung by the office and picked up bolt cutters before heading north on Highway 3 towards Gustavus Island. Under normal circumstances Inspector Gilbert didn't want his detectives executing search warrants alone, but these, Irene told herself, were not normal circumstances. For one thing, vacations had left the department depleted, and the remaining officers were swamped with their own work, leaving no logical candidate to accompany her on a search of premises that in all likelihood weren't linked in any way to whatever had befallen Anne Paris. If asked to justify her interest, Irene wouldn't have been able to offer anything more substantial than curiosity aroused by proximity—a death, a stranger on the beach, a cabin that wasn't his, and nearby a boat run aground. Anyway, Inspector Gilbert himself had left on his own vacation and wasn't going to hear about what she was up to in his absence.

Research the previous afternoon had ascertained that the cabin and the narrow strip of land it sat on were owned by the now middle-aged niece of the man who had built it several decades before. Stationed in Florida, the current owner, Staff Sergeant Celeste Donley, a career army officer, had registered little surprise at the news that a squatter seemed to be utilizing the cabin she had inherited from her uncle. It wasn't the first time, Sergeant Donley reported. It had been broken into many times and anything worth stealing had long since been taken. It was unplumbed, not wired, mildewed and spider infested. She herself hadn't been there in years, had no plans to visit, would sell the property in a heartbeat if there were a taker, and the Mason County Sheriff's Department could carry on however it saw fit. She was gratified that anyone cared. Irene saw no need to reveal the fact that her interest in investigating was tangential to any potential property rights infraction that might be going on.

Irene drove with the window open. High up the jet stream was pulling a thin scrim of mare's tails across the early morning sun. She turned off 3 onto the Pickering Road and cruised through the collection of trailers and cottages which, together with a tavern, a drive-through espresso slash drop-ins welcome chiropractor and a couple of gas pumps, made up the community of Spencer Lake. Some miles further, at a fork in the road where she swung left for the bridge, a hand-painted sandwich board advertised the upcoming Gustavus Island dance held every year on the Saturday before Labor Day at the Grange Hall, an annual headache for the Mason County sheriff's deputies patrolling the highways.

It was a deceptively wholesome occasion, a throwback to an earlier era when generations mingled. Early in the evening little kids chased each other around until they captured a partner, then gravely rendered arm-pumping fox-trots in imitation of their parents, while a few elderly couples dipped and twirled with clockwork precision. Summer residents attended wearing sophisticated black, and executed intricate lindy and salsa moves to the band's mix of country and fifties rock. The Grange ladies sold coffee and pie and there was no alcohol served, but as the night wore on the families thinned out, replaced by carloads of teenagers, loggers, and mill workers who drove out from Shelton and Union and Allyn to stomp and gyrate suggestively without ever holding onto their partners. Between numbers and during breaks the new arrivals trooped out to drink beer, clustering around coolers in the backs of pickups and the trunks of cars. There were sometimes fights in the parking lot and often accidents along the two-lane roads in the midnight aftermath of the Grange Hall dance. Tight corners along the county thoroughfares were marked with white crosses and homemade shrines.

This morning, though, there was little traffic. Once on the island, the road meandered along the shoreline for a while, then cut inland following the section lines. Straightaways ran between tracts of Douglas fir, then changed direction in alarming ninety degree turns. At one of these bends in the road—a blind corner where visibility was obscured by trees and undergrowth crowding the verge—Irene was nearly sideswiped as a car traveling in the opposite direction swung wide taking the turn. It was an easy mistake to make: empty roads, a little too much speed and an unexpectedly tight radius on the curve. The moment of danger passed but the rush of adrenaline preserved the instant.

As Irene came out of the turn the image of the other driver was burned onto the back of her retinas, their eyes meeting for a fraction of a second, his face only feet from hers as they passed. It was the face of the bearded man on the beach.

In a single practiced motion Irene braked and hit her grill lights while swinging the wheel, sending the Crown Vic into a sideways skid, reversing direction. But even so she had to back up and maneuver to complete a U-turn in the narrow roadway, and rounding the curve again, accelerating in pursuit, she saw the other car. She gunned it but she wouldn't catch him, she'd lost too much time and he was flying. By the time she rounded the next bend he was no longer in sight. She radioed in a report of a late-model silver Camry on Gustavus Island speeding toward the bridge, so that out on 3 and 101 the patrol officers would be keeping an eye out; but Irene hadn't gotten any part of the license number and it was the most generic of cars. Absent an obvious infraction he wouldn't be pulled over.

Irene wondered if he'd registered the Crown Vic as an unmarked police car, seen her blue lights flashing in his rearview mirror. She thought it was unlikely.

THE CABIN in the woods, once she arrived, was deserted. It was unlocked, the padlock gone. No need for the bolt cutters. All evidence of habitation had vanished. She walked in and flopped into the pink mohair armchair and looked around, frustrated. She felt quite certain, though she knew she was assuming—something she tried not to do—that it was the man on the beach, the man in the car at the corner, who had been the cabin's occupant. And where was he off to in such a hurry? It was a fluke of timing. Just minutes earlier and she'd have run into him on the overgrown track that led in to the cabin, too narrow for his car to have passed hers. She'd have known then who he was and what he'd been doing here.

The woods in Mason County might seem primordial as one walked alone, but in fact there was little old timber left. All the woods had been cut at one time or another, and what grew now was in essence a crop. But in the leisurely interval between sapling and harvest, the vast untended Douglas fir forests provided a habitat for wildlife and illegal subcultures. Most prevalent and benign were brush cutters and mushroomers—mostly foreigners from Mexico or Cambodia or other agrarian Third World countries who slipped into the woods with baskets and machetes to cut salal and huckleberry for the floral industry, and to pick chanterelle and lobster mushrooms in the fall and morels in the spring to sell to restaurants and at farmers' markets. They were furtive and elusive but not dangerous. More menacing were the backwoods' chemists who hauled travel trailers and propane tanks deep into the forests where they cooked methamphetamines, side arms at the ready and attack dogs on patrol. They moved often, leaving behind squalid evidence of their activity: unburned trash, beer cans and the wrappings of thousands of Sudafed tablets. Her guy, Irene thought, fit neither category.

Early morning sun flooded in through the east-facing windows. She could, she thought, doze briefly in the comfort of the ancient armchair.

⌘

WHEN SHE snapped awake not much time had passed. She sat still, listening. Something had awakened her. Then in an instant she was on her feet, yanking open the firebox of the wood-burning range. Papers were smoldering inside, making small pops and crackles. That was what she'd heard. The rush of entering air rekindled the fire and Irene slammed the door shut and fumbled for the damper on the stove pipe. She kicked herself for her stupidity. She should have thought to investigate the stove immediately.

She looked around and located a lid lifter, and when she checked again the fire had subsided, though there was little left but ash. What had been burning seemed to have been a crumpled grocery bag containing papers and trash. Irene poked gingerly through fragile flakes of ash, but all that was identifiable was part of a Special K box and the charred remains of a panty liner.

It only took moments to search the rest of the cabin. A grocery bag behind the stove contained what appeared to be recycling, from which Irene could surmise a diet of sardines, chili, and cheap red wine, though there was one heavy, dark bottle with the label soaked off. In the sleeping loft above there was a candle on the windowsill, and on the far side of the mattress, slipped down against the stud wall, Irene found a fuchsia-colored cotton thong and a recent issue of *The New Yorker* magazine with a yellow forwarding label addressed to Oliver Paris MD on the Fergus Point Road.

Irene sat on the mattress and flipped through the magazine. Arts and politics and enigmatic cartoons. Irene wondered if *The New Yorker* had been filched out of Oliver Paris's mailbox by the departed squatter, or if Anne could have brought it here—or Nikki or Libby or one of the Strauss wives, or anyone else for that matter. But she was picturing Anne, like a latter day Goldilocks, walking through the woods and coming upon this cabin, climbing the ladder to this loft and making love here on this mattress with the now vanished interloper, then sitting side-by-side with him in the bed, reading together. The image was oddly domestic—Anne Paris perusing her father's *New Yorker* by candlelight in the company of the bearded stranger.

Who was he, wondered Irene, and why had he fled? In her years of police work Irene had learned that things were usually as they seemed, it was the accurate interpretation of the what-seems-to-be that was elusive. What looked like flight could possibly be nothing more than the rush to keep an appointment or the normal behavior of a driver with a lead foot. Also, the imagined consequence which inspired seemingly guilty behavior could range across an enormous spectrum. A shoplifter might exhibit a murderer's desperation. So to extrapolate culpability—or even knowledge—regarding Anne's death from this man's proximity and his precipitous departure, though tempting, was surely not the only way to read the little information Irene possessed.

Irene tried to think of what she knew for sure. Anne had been out sailing late on Saturday evening in the I-14 when a squall hit. The I-14 had capsized and had run aground on the beach not far below where Irene now sat, though the body was found miles north of here in the slough. Anne hadn't drowned but she had inhaled some salt water. Death had come from a blow to the back of the head inflicted by an irregularly shaped blunt object. Anne's relationship with her boyfriend was rocky. She was the apple of her father's eye, the envy of her sister.

It would be interesting to find out the disposition of the considerable property belonging to Dr. Paris in the event of his death. Anne's death might significantly change the future prospects of Leland and Libby.

And now this evidence, or suggestion anyway, that there might be another man, someone else figuring in the romantic landscape of Anne's world. Greed and jealousy, as everyone knew, were the most likely motivators of violent acts.

There were, Irene decided, conversations she must continue with the Paris family and their guests. But sitting in the warm sunshine in the decrepit Donley cabin Irene felt doped and dull. There was no edge to her thinking. Dorothy in the field of poppies, powerless to resist the allure of slumber. She lay back on the mattress in the sun-drenched sleeping loft while flies bumbled lazily against the windowpanes.

XII

Alsatians were old-fashioned dogs, Irene thought, voguish in the middle of the last century—war dogs, police dogs, guide dogs—their popularity leading to over-breeding and genetic hip deformities. Poor Gus, Mr. Guevara's German shepherd, ferocious black-masked head and threatening growl notwithstanding, wobbled on wasted hindquarters beside his owner's left leg.

Standing on the verandah of the Guevara house looking out toward the Sound, you looked directly across the Paris slough. "It was a mistake, pure and simple," Mr. Guevara was saying. "You can see, standing here, that if you ran the lot lines down to the water, that slough is mine. Ninety percent of it."

"I don't buy it," said Irene. "You're an attorney. Attorneys don't make mistakes like that."

"You overestimate me, Detective," he said. "I was in love with that slough. I fell in love at first sight. Two years ago I stood exactly here, where we are now, in tall grass, no house, nothing, in the middle of twenty-seven enviable acres, and I looked out over all of this"—he swept an arm expansively north to south—"and I made a full price offer on the spot. My realtor blanched. It was impetuous, yes. Emotional, yes. And uncharacteristic, you're right. I assumed—a mistake clients make, not me—I *assumed* that the lot lines *did* continue straight to the water and I *assumed* that the slough was mine along with the beach in front of it. It never crossed my mind it wasn't until one morning there appears a post sunk into the middle of my path down there on the dune with a

NO TRESPASSING sign nailed to it. *My* path. You have to understand that's how I viewed it."

The survey, Irene had determined, which had occurred the afternoon after the discovery of Anne's body—only yesterday!—had been scheduled some time back, so the coincidence of timing was only that. A coincidence.

Mr. Guevara had shown her on the survey map, the way the Paris property line extended along the back side of the slough, running in front of his own property in an elongated triangle until it met the Sound. It was true that this seemed incongruous with the rectilinear geometry of the plats. Irene could see the plausibility of the mistake he described. But she was not wholly convinced.

"What's the right of adverse possession?" she asked.

Mr. Guevara swung around to look at her directly. "Is that what they're saying?" Irene didn't answer and he turned again to the vista of lawn giving way to reeds ringing the slough, then the narrow isthmus of dune and beach and the Sound beyond. He shook his head wonderingly. After a moment he said, "You know, I was gearing up for a fight. That's why I ordered the survey. I thought *they* were going to claim the right of adverse possession. They've been here since forever, you know, walking out there, picnicking, swimming. Isn't that funny," he said rhetorically. "Not many people know about that law."

"Why did you take the wine up there yesterday?" Irene asked.

"Well, because of the survey, of course," he replied. "I was conceding. I mean, you know, one thing about the practice of law, one doesn't always win. I'm no stranger to losing, dear girl—though mind you, I'm more accustomed to winning," he amended quickly, glancing her way.

Irene smiled. Dear girl. It was like being addressed in a Victorian novel as gentle reader. So quaintly condescending as to be endearing.

"I was absolutely certain," he went on, "that the slough was mine. And the survey has demonstrated absolutely that it isn't. A devastating loss, but one adjusts, you know. It's an esthetic asset after all and one I can possess without owning. I mean, it's my view, it's what I see. It's the look of the place I value, the way the water reflects the sky, the changing seasons, the color of the reeds, the waterfowl it attracts. It's highly personal. You might not grasp that notion," he added.

"Maybe not," agreed Irene, though she thought she did. She liked the look of it too, more gloomy and brooding than the bright water of the Sound.

"Yesterday," she said, "when you took them the wine, you didn't go out to the road and walk down their drive, you walked out across the disputed stretch of beach and up their orchard path."

"Indeed," he said.

"Why?" she asked.

"Why not?" he countered. "It was a neighborly visit."

What a fox, she thought. Conceding, yes, but assertive in his neighborliness. "And you offered condolences," she said.

"Well, of course," he said. "They've just had this ghastly loss. I'm a practical man, Detective Chavez, not heartless. Cold, some might say, but they'd be wrong—I too have feelings."

"Where did you get the wine?" Irene asked.

He turned, looking directly at her. "What an astonishing question," he said, "Why ever do you ask?"

Irene didn't answer.

"That was a very elegant bottle of wine," he said. "It didn't come from Safeway."

"I presumed not," said Irene. "Where did you get it?"

"McCarthy and Shiering perhaps," he said after a moment, "up in Seattle. Queen Anne Hill. But I no longer recall. I buy a lot of wine. Living out here one keeps a bit of a cellar. I went down to the cellar and chose something I thought he'd like."

Driving down the Fergus Point Road, Irene had overtaken Mr. Guevara walking with Gus at his side. She'd slowed and stopped and had left her car at the junction where his driveway met the road in order to accompany him on foot as he continued down the long, meandering approach to his house.

She felt addled and inept, having awakened from a troubled sleep in the warm loft of the Donley cabin where she had dreamt of being pursued through an entangling forest by the man from the beach. Branches reached out, tripping her, and she tumbled into a thicket where she lay hidden, her heart thudding as she watched him pass. She wanted to shoot but was afraid to move. Then her gun was in her hands and she was drawing a bead on the back of his head. He turned around and it wasn't the man from the beach at all, but a seal looking reproachfully over its shoulder at her. Then the scene shifted and she was on the beach aiming her pistol at the seal out in the water. Dr. Paris was running toward her shouting, "No!" Startled, she turned her head and as she did so the gun leapt in her hands, there was a report and a crimson eruption in the water where the seal had been. Irene woke in a sweat.

Even now, she couldn't quite shake the residue of guilt and unease left by the dream. She had seized the opportunity which the encounter with Mr. Guevara provided to delay once again her inquiries into the Paris family. Irene wondered if she were getting sick. Maybe a sinus infection would account for this feeling of imbalance. She thought again of Dorothy overcome in the field of poppies. She had to pull herself together.

"Do you mind if I sit down a moment?" Irene asked. Behind where they were standing an inviting row of wicker chairs was lined up along the verandah.

Mr. Guevara turned and studied her. "My dear, of course not. You must come in," he said, and took her by the elbow and guided her along the verandah and through open French doors into the house. The living room was like a hotel lobby, populated with a grand piano and groupings of large, chintz-covered furniture. He led her to a chair in the corner of the room where a massive telescope was positioned next to the window.

"Tea, Detective Chavez?" he asked, "or coffee? I make a lovely espresso."

"Oh, yes," said Irene. "Coffee would be great."

Released from his leash, Gus climbed onto a sofa, turned in a circle and collapsed with his chin on the cushioned arm.

After a few minutes Mr. Guevara reappeared carrying Italian demitasse on a silver tray. He sat opposite her and Irene took the cup he offered in both her hands, breathing in the steam and aroma. In spite of herself, she was disarmed by his solicitude. She couldn't think when she'd last felt so looked after. He might, she thought, studying him, be close to seventy. And still a handsome man, olive-skinned with a patrician nose and a flat, wide mouth. Maybe something of the Aztec in him. He was wearing a light cotton safari jacket over a blue oxford shirt, khaki pants, and leather fisherman's sandals. He had taken off the Panama hat as he came indoors and she noticed that his thinning gray hair was combed back and caught into a short, sparse ponytail, which surprised her. He seemed in other respects a thoroughly conventional man. A ceiling fan circulated slowly, stirring the air.

"What do you look at?" she asked, indicating the telescope.

"This time of year, the Pleiades. Spectacular meteor showers in the Pleiades each August. The moons of Jupiter. If it's clear one has good viewing here. There's not much ambient light."

"May I take a look?" Irene asked.

"Well, you may, but there's nothing to see. One has to wait until dark."

Even so, Irene moved to a straight-backed chair and bent her head to the view-finder of the telescope. It was true that she saw nothing in the heavens except gauzy blue. But when she tilted the telescope downward and adjusted the knob, the trees on the Long Branch Peninsula opposite jumped into focus. She raised her head and looked at him.

"Were you able," Irene asked, "to see Anne sailing on Saturday evening?"

"I watched her go out, yes," Mr. Guevara replied carefully. "She paddled out in a canoe, tied up to the buoy and clambered aboard the sailboat. I've watched her often. It's the neighborly thing to do."

"How so?" asked Irene.

There was a silence while Mr. Guevara seemed to consider what to say next. "There used to be," he began, "years ago— many years ago—a house here on this site. House perhaps is the wrong word. A cabin. A handmade A-frame." He looked at her. "Have you heard this story?"

"No."

"It might surprise you to know that I've become acquainted with the year-rounders here. I am myself a year-rounder, when it comes down to it. The Paris family and the Strausses, all the summer people, they're standoffish, exclusive. They don't mingle. But I'm retired, I live here full time. And I've embraced life down here. I'm one of them now, to some degree. I'm interested, you see, and I inquire. People tell me things. History. Gossip. Oliver Paris, for instance, wouldn't think a thing of it if he saw Jill Wozniak from up the road headed to town driving the pickup, her husband Roy riding shotgun. I happen to know, though, that Roy's spitting nails. He can't stand it. Jill's behind the wheel because Roy's license was suspended back in April when he got pulled over and refused a Breathalyzer." He looked at Irene. "As law enforcement you might know that, of course, or surmise it."

Irene laughed. "Maybe."

"But the story I want to tell you," he went on, "is something else. In the forties there was a house just about here, a summer house, owned by the Gillettes, a family from Seattle. One August evening that family sat on the bluff here on the porch in front of their cabin and watched while their teenaged son went out sailing. A wind comes up. The sky darkens and the water changes color. Far out they watch the sail race and dip—then vanish. There's no phone, no other vessel to paddle or row to the rescue, no way to summon help. There's nothing they can do. From this perfect vantage they are an audience to their son's drowning." Mr. Guevara paused. He looked, Irene thought, quite stricken.

After a moment he continued. "The house fell into disrepair— haunted, people said—and eventually it burned to the ground. Arson? More bad luck? No one knows. The Gillette family never returned. The land stood vacant until I came along. Some people said I was foolish to buy, that there was a jinx." Mr. Guevara turned and looked at Irene. "I'm sure it could be interpreted as bizarre in its way and not very wholesome, certainly out of character, but, yes, I watched Anne. I watched her often. It felt like a duty that had somehow fallen to me, that had come with the territory, an obligation to watch over her. I was afraid of the jinx.

"In fact, I knew her," he added after a moment. "You may not know that," checking her reaction. Irene kept her face neutral and he continued. "She was cordial. Not like her father. There have been occasions when we've spoken. You know, I'd see her on the road or on the beach. She introduced herself. Very straightforward, very charming. Lovely. She's come to the house and sat here, like you. I was captivated." Mr. Guevara looked at Irene. "And yes, I watched her sailing on Saturday evening. I have a skiff down there on my buoy and I always felt that if something untoward were to happen, I would be able to help."

"On Saturday evening did you see anything untoward happen?" asked Irene.

"No," he said. "Whatever happened, happened out of my sight. She tacked back and forth for a while out here where I could see her, then sailed south, wing on wing, flying before the wind, and disappeared behind the land mass of Fergus Point."

"What's wing on wing?" Irene asked.

"The jib's out to one side and the mainsail on the other. You can only do that sailing directly ahead of the wind."

"Was she alone?"

"Oh, yes," he said without hesitation.

"Did you think she was in trouble or having trouble or that anything was amiss?"

"No," he said. "If I had, I'd have done something." He was quiet a moment then added, "But it was a very big wind."

Mr. Guevara had placed a strip of lemon peel on her saucer and Irene twisted it over her cup and watched the atomized oil film the surface of her espresso. "When Anne came here to the house did she talk about the property dispute?" she asked.

"No."

"What did she talk about?"

"She was having difficulties with her boyfriend."

"What did she have to say about that?"

"He had been unfaithful and she was quite sad and affronted." Saying this, Mr. Guevara sounded affronted himself, as though he too were wronged by Ira's Ecuadorian affair.

"Did her father know she was coming here?" asked Irene.

"I never asked but I presume not," he said. "Anne was lonely and at a very vulnerable moment, and she was drawn to me," he went on, "but you have to understand, she was a good deal younger and there was no impropriety. She confided in me, that's all." He closed his eyes and pinched the bridge of his nose. "To tell you the truth," he said, "I'm quite devastated."

XIII

Walking back to where she'd left her car, Irene mused about the clandestine friendship between the patrician Puerto Rican attorney and the alluring young doctor, of which Oliver Paris would surely not have approved. Nor, Irene thought, would Mr. Guevara be pleased to learn what she herself now surmised about an interloper in the Donley cabin and Anne's presence there. To Irene it seemed vaguely Shakespearian, two old men feuding over an acre of water and a useless isthmus of land, both besotted with the duplicitous Anne, and meanwhile all manner of subplots playing out in the forest. She wondered if Ira knew or cared.

⚜

D<small>R</small>. P<small>ARIS</small> was not in his study. Irene tapped and when there was no answer she pushed the door open and looked in. His chair was empty, the room vacant, the table top bare. She looked at her watch. Her day had started early and she'd lost track of time but it wasn't yet eleven. The coffee had helped—Mr. Guevara indeed made a lovely espresso—and she was feeling more herself, alert and curious now as to the whereabouts of the doctor, whose schedule, she had been led to believe, even in grief, was inviolate.

At the house, when Irene asked to see the doctor, Yvonne protested in a long string of excited French, out of which Irene deciphered *non, non, non!* and *dormer*, hands to cheek miming sleep. *"Si,"* said Irene firmly, Spanish being the only foreign language she knew at all, and flashed her badge in a muscular show, which was successful in persuading Yvonne to lead her up the narrow stairs.

The original farmhouse had been enlarged over the years by lean-to additions which had created the kitchen, a back bedroom and the long porch which housed the bathroom and woodshed; but the old part of the house consisted of four rooms: two tall downstairs rooms, now a living room and a dining room, and above, two bedrooms on opposite sides of a small sunlit landing.

Irene had been here before. On the first day of the investigation she had searched Anne's room, a plain white room with a pumpkin yellow floor, a brass bed and otherwise unremarkable old furniture. Irene had looked in drawers, flipped through books, investigated the contents of the wastebasket. She'd flung back the sheets, searched beneath the mattress, emptied the pockets of all the pants, jackets, and shorts hung in the closet or strewn on the chair. She therefore had known without being told, among other things, that Anne smoked. There were half-empty packs of Camel Lights in the pockets of a Levi jacket and a pair of shorts. And another in the back of a small top drawer of a tallboy chest where Anne kept her underwear—thongs like the one in the Donley loft mingled with prim white cotton briefs. A satin pouch contained amethyst earrings, a double strand of gray freshwater pearls, and an astonishingly large diamond in a platinum setting in a turquoise Tiffany's box. Who, Irene wondered, had bestowed that?

Irene knew Anne took birth control pills and wore hospital scrubs for pajama pants. She wasn't tidy. Her shoes were finely made and size nine. Her nightstand was cluttered with textbooks and professional journals, but the August *Vogue* was on top of the stack. Irene dropped prescription vials containing Flagyl and Xanax into an evidence bag. In an old-fashioned drop front desk she found stamps, string, some letterhead engraved with an outdated Cambridge address, crayons, paper clips, a roll of unprocessed thirty-five millimeter film—which Irene also confiscated, a book of matches from the Spencer Lake Tavern, and a sheaf of labels soaked off of wine bottles. A wooden trunk under the window contained Clue and Monopoly, Bicycle playing cards, a box of plastic poker chips, a mayonnaise jar full of beach glass, and a stack of letters and postcards in rubber bands, which Irene also took. Anne's handbag, a massive Botega Veneta affair of woven leather, a kind of quintessential repository holding everything from sunscreen and a zippered cosmetics bag to file folders of patient records, a bulging Daytimer, wallet, and passport—Anne's face tilted slightly, smiling directly into the camera—Irene took in its entirety.

As Yvonne tapped on the door opposite, Irene reminded herself she must find time for a more detailed scrutiny of the confiscated items. By now the lab would have processed the film and the photos would be awaiting her attention.

⋙⋘

WHEN THERE was no response to Yvonne's timid knocking, Irene shouldered her aside and rapped sharply before opening the closed door and stepping in, pulling the door to behind her. In contrast to the bright landing the room was dim behind drawn shades. As her eyes adjusted Irene made out Dr. Paris supine on the bed, lying fully dressed on top of the coverlet, a black handkerchief tied around his eyes. He looked like a corpse, the victim of an execution, but one long white hand flapped at the interruption. "What?" he asked, "Who's there?"

"Dr. Paris," said Irene, "it's me, Irene Chavez." As soon as she uttered the words, she realized the grammatical mistake. It is I, she should have said. This, she thought, was what was wrong with her whole entire investigation—these people reminded her of who she was and where she'd come from, a sawyer's daughter from a backwater mill town. Get over it, she scolded herself. No good cop could afford to be impressed by anyone's standing in the world or education or sophistication.

"I have nothing to add to what you already know," Dr. Paris said, "and I'm suffering at the moment from a migraine. This isn't a good time for an interview. Noise disturbs me and I must remain perfectly still or I'll vomit."

"Well," said Irene, tapping into a well of resolve, "sometimes no time is a good time for an interview. I'll talk softly and you don't have to move. I don't have a whole lot of questions anyway."

Her phone was vibrating against her hip but Irene ignored it. Whatever it was, it could wait. She had interrogated Dr. Paris briefly on the first day. Just the standard protocol of when did you see her last, did she seem despondent, any reason to think anyone might mean her harm. He had provided no useful information then, but even so she needed to follow up. She wondered why he was so reluctant to talk to her. Most people close to an unexpected death pressured and badgered for theories and developments.

"I don't think your daughter died by accident," Irene said bluntly.

Silence from the bed.

"She didn't drown, and the head injury that killed her is inconsistent with the boom of the sailboat," Irene went on, "We've ascertained that."

"How can you tell?" he asked.

"Forensics can tell," she said, "the coroner and medical examiner. They look at the wound and they look at the boom. You know that, you're a doctor."

"Maybe she fell."

"Maybe," said Irene dubiously. "But you've still got to wonder how it is that her body wound up in the slough. The boat was found two miles south."

"A southerly wind on an incoming tide."

"The wind was from the north," said Irene.

"It's incomprehensible that she's gone," said Dr. Paris after a moment, "completely implausible that she won't be coming through the door. You're young, Detective Chavez. You have no idea what it means to lose someone"—Irene stifled the impulse to set him straight on this point—"but do you have any concept of how little I care about the particulars of her death? She's gone. The light of my life."

"If she was killed, don't you care by whom?" Grammatically correct this time.

"Not really," he said. "What does it change?"

Irene tried to imagine circumstances in which a father wouldn't want to know. As a wife, *she* had wanted to know. For years as she'd driven Ventura Boulevard, she'd looked at the faces of boys and men hanging out on the street corners and wondered if they were the ones. Sometimes during an arrest or an interrogation, out of the blue she'd lean into someone's face demanding, "What do you know about a guy who got jumped at the CitiBank ATM on Van Nuys?" Her partners got used to it and just stood back and looked away when she went down that road. Sometimes another officer yanked her off and shoved her into the hall saying, "Chill." Sometimes she scared a kid into confessing to something entirely unrelated. The fury that in those years boiled just under the surface eventually subsided, replaced by grief and later resignation—just like in the books, she thought, the stages of loss. But even now Irene sometimes wondered if whoever had done it was ever troubled by remorse—somewhere in the world someone else besides her lying awake at night thinking about Luis—or troubled by other kinds of consequences that having gotten away with murder might have on a person. Not knowing had made her wary: any random stranger might hide terrible secrets. She was alert and suspicious. Good qualities in a cop. But knowing what she knew about criminal behavior, Irene could make the assumption that by now Luis's killers were likely dead themselves or in jail for some other crime.

Luis's death was senseless but impersonal. But if Irene was right, Anne had known her killer. "Who had reason to mean her harm?" Irene asked.

"Reason? No one. Everyone loved her."

"When you say everyone, who do you mean?" asked Irene.

"I mean everyone. Ask anyone."

"Ira?"

"Ira, yes." But there was a hesitation.

"They were on the outs, weren't they?"

"I don't know," he said. "Some strain perhaps."

"Libby?"

"Libby, yes."

"And Leland?"

"Of course."

"What does your will say about your estate? Won't Libby and Leland benefit by Anne's demise?"

A chilly pause. "Only time will tell you that," he said.

"So what," said Irene, "it's all going to the Make-A-Wish Foundation?"

"This is not a subject I'll discuss with you or anyone."

"What about Mr. Guevara?" asked Irene, frustrated.

"What about Mr. Guevara?" asked Dr. Paris. "Mr. Guevara had reason to dislike me but he didn't even *know* Anne."

"I've got news for you," said Irene.

Dr. Paris pushed the handkerchief up onto his forehead and hitched up on his pillow, looking at her. Now that he was sitting up it was harder to bully him. His face was pale and slack, his pupils dilated.

"You may not care about the particulars, Dr. Paris, but I do," said Irene. "The law does. My supervisor is going to come back from vacation and close the case and call it accidental if I'm not able to give him some compelling reason not to. Is that what you want?"

"Suits me," he said.

"Maybe too many people loved her," Irene said, taking another tack.

"What does that mean?" he asked.

"Who's the man squatting in the Donley cabin?"

"I haven't the faintest idea what you're talking about."

"Someone's broken into the Donley cabin down the beach and was living there."

"And so?"

"Anne's been there."

"I don't believe that, but what of it?"

"Well," said Irene, "I'm not going to argue, but I found your *New Yorker* there," she said, pulling the folded magazine out of her hip pocket, flattening it and putting it on his bedside table. Dr. Paris was silent.

"There was a ring among her things," she said, "a big diamond from Tiffany's. Is that from Ira or who? Whom?" correcting herself.

"Maybe my mother's," he said.

"So not an engagement ring?" asked Irene.

"My mother had a diamond," he said, "but I don't think you'd say it was big. Just a little chip of a diamond in a plain gold setting that my father gave her before they were married. A long time ago. When Mother died I let Anne have it."

"Not the same ring," she said. "This one is big and set in platinum. Was she engaged, do you know?"

"No one asked permission of me," he answered.

"Is that something you'd expect?" she asked.

He gave her a look that answered the question. Oliver Paris would indeed expect a formal request for his permission and blessing by anyone who wished to marry his daughter.

"Well, Ira Logan is broke," Irene said, "it isn't from him. Was there some suitor before Ira who might have given her a ring? I mean, is this an artifact from some previous relationship?"

"Detective Chavez," he said, "I don't know what ring you're talking about. I've never seen such a ring so I have no idea where it came from or how she got it or under what circumstances or with what understanding."

Irene was frustrated by Dr. Paris's impenetrability, and at the same time the unwelcome thought of Victor and his long empty summer days was intruding on her focus. What was he doing now? Where was he? His work schedule at the market and his lawn-mowing obligations were noted on a calendar stuck to the refrigerator, but she didn't have any of it in mind. She wondered who it was who'd called and if there was a message on her phone. Her interview with Dr. Paris was going nowhere and she wanted to call home.

XIV

"Theo Choate, prosecuting attorney," the message said tersely—tightening a band of anxiety around Irene's chest—along with the county number and an extension to call.

Out on Highway 3 headed back to town, she got a signal and left a message with the secretary—Mr. Choate was in court—saying that she'd be in her office through the afternoon. It was not a good sign, she thought, that he was so on top of Victor's minor infraction. She had hoped he'd lob it right back down the hill into the municipal court where it belonged, if it belonged anywhere. New in the job and overly zealous, she feared.

Her anxiety eased incrementally in town when she detoured to swing past the corner market and saw Victor's bike locked up outside. Accounted for, for now at least.

⁂

HER DESK, when she got there, was piled with paperwork. Everyone who had done anything on the case on the first day, when they were all out on Gustavus Island, had funneled their documentation to her. Department procedure required that everyone take notes of whatever they did on any aspect of an investigation. All the witness statements, handwritten or tape-recorded and transcribed, along with each deputy's narrative of events and an inventory from the evidence department, had found their way to her. Normally, on a potential homicide case Inspector Gilbert would be reviewing everything, but since he was away on vacation, Irene was on her own. Lead on this one. Solo, in fact, on this one.

It would, she thought, be a good use of her afternoon to sift through all the material produced thus far. Try to impose some system and order onto the chaos churning in her head and piled on her desk.

She started with her own photographs, overlapping the ends of the images to create panoramas and pinning them at eye level on the partition next to her desk. When she was done she stood back. These kind of composite panoramas weren't realistic because they captured more than the thirty-five degrees the human eye took in; and unlike a photo taken by a wide angle lens, there was no fish-bowl distortion. Like cinemascope they suggested a surreally vast landscape. Unless you knew you were looking at a crime scene, you wouldn't make out the body floating at the edge of the slough in the center of her first panorama. You wouldn't know what the thing in the water was. You'd take it for a log and look instead to the left at the orchard, the gnarled old trees, gray with lichen and heavy with fruit.

Next was the sequence she'd shot standing on the dune and looking inland, showing on one side the phalanx of volunteer fire personnel with Rosalie in the lead approaching through the orchard, then the slough and on the other side the Guevara mansion. Then the sequence she'd taken facing the other way, out toward the Sound. And last, a close-up panorama that included the tips of her own boots, which showed the cigarette butt she remembered seeing in the grass. She had collected that butt and it was now secured in the evidence locker. Someone's DNA was on that butt, if things ever progressed far enough for that to matter.

Irene was pleased. Her photography did what she had intended—it drew her back into the first moments before she had learned anything or developed any theories.

The roll of thirty-five millimeter film Irene had found in Anne's desk turned out to be disappointing, snapshots from some previous summer—Owen and Neal at younger ages and Julia Paris, a strangely beautiful woman, chiseled cheeks and haunting, hooded eyes—photos taken on the beach on some forgotten cloudy afternoon. Oliver on the dune in a beach chair reading.

Irene shuffled through the sheaf of soaked-off wine labels. Some of the collection had notations in pencil on the back, dates and descriptions—'nice tannins, full-bodied, earthy'—and the occasion when it was served—'my birthday'—or a serving suggestion— 'good with paella'—and the name of the person who provided it or shared it—'Daddy' 'Nigel' 'Leland,' or names Irene didn't recognize—'Otto' 'Storey'—guests perhaps from past summers. Among the labels was a 1982 Latour à Pomerol. No notation to enlighten Irene as to when it was drunk, on what occasion or with whom, but she wondered if this might be the label belonging to the bottle she'd discovered in the Donley cabin; and if it might be the one that had gone missing from Oliver's crate in the barn, purloined perhaps by Dr. Paris's own daughter, its absence now making her father anxious and paranoid.

The initial investigation of Anne's laptop had turned up almost nothing. She hadn't had internet reception since she'd left Boston, except for one occasion when apparently she'd connected from somewhere in Shelton that had Wi-Fi, and had read and responded to her email. Nothing jumped out at Irene as interesting or helpful. There were a lot of messages, a lot of it spam. She read a couple of messages in their entirety from Nikki, who had arrived some days after the Paris family, and who was asking about logistics—should she rent a car or would she be picked up—and wondering 'how *are* you, darling?' And one from the landlord, Julian Bernstein complaining that he had not heard from her and wondering 'how things stand.' The unpaid rent.

There was a printout of some patient notes—the patient identified only by initials—and an outline and some narrative paragraphs that appeared to be the beginning of a paper Anne was writing, having to do with the treatment of certain kinds of pathologies.

Felix Guzmán's report held no surprises. Cause of death was blunt trauma to the back of the head and nothing else noteworthy was contained in the initial findings. Later, when results came back from tissue samples and lab reports, maybe they'd learn she'd taken a Xanax or there was a lesion in her lung, or a faulty heart valve—but there would be nothing that would change anything for Irene's purposes.

Dr. Paris had opposed the autopsy and tried to block it. Irene knew what an autopsy entailed—any physician would too, and Dr. Paris was a physician—it was a gruesome and irreverent process. It left the body of the deceased eviscerated, all the organs removed, sectioned for slides, then stuffed back in willy-nilly to fill out the vacant cavities, the cadaver stitched and stapled closed and left to the mortician to make presentable.

⁂

A couple of hours later, Irene was tilted back in her chair with her feet on her desk, contemplating her photo montages and digesting the material she'd been reading, when her intercom beeped and Wanda, the receptionist, announced Theo Choate. Irene walked out to meet him and ushered him back to her office.

Prosecutors didn't last long in this part of the state. Almost no one came here on purpose. The pay was low, culture was absent, and if you had an option, you'd take it. Or at least that was the general perception. So Irene, reaching to shake his hand, wondered what had brought Theo Choate to the backwater of Mason County. Early forties, she thought, a well-cut suit hanging nicely on a lean frame, markedly more polished than the last couple of prosecutors. She led him back through the warren of partitions.

⁂

In point of fact, Mason County appealed to Theo Choate. He had grown up in the Berkshires in western Massachusetts, related in a distant way to the distinguished Choates who had spawned, among other things, the eponymous prep school, which Theo had not attended. He'd gone to the local high school, failed to get into the Ivy League—disappointing family aspirations—gone to the state university instead, and then gotten a low-rent law degree in upstate New York, joined an Albany firm and married a partner. Corporate law was not a good fit, and when the marriage ended he pulled up stakes and moved to the furthest reaches of the continent, to Sitka in southeast Alaska where he bought into a fishing boat and plied the depleted waters each summer for halibut and salmon, and crabbed through the winters. It was a ferocious life in a dwindling fishery, and before too many years Theo bought out his discouraged partner and a few years later threw in the towel himself, sold his fishing shares and moved down to the lower forty-eight. When he passed the Washington State bar exam, Theo wasn't looking for much more than a living in a career where he wouldn't throw out his back or lose a finger to a line or go down in icy seas.

⌘

"WHAT CAN I do for you, Mr. Choate?" Irene asked once back in her cubicle.

"Theo," he said, "I don't stand too much on formality, Detective."

"Well then, Irene."

He smiled. "I'm just kind of introducing myself around, getting to know folks"—and for a tiny elated moment Irene thought this wasn't going to be about Victor at all, but then he went on—"and your name kind of percolated to the top of my list."

"How's that?" she asked, instantly prickly and defensive.

Silence and a faint, skeptical smile.

"Don't you have better things to do?" Irene asked finally.

"I'm not sure I do," he said levelly. "When I came on I made kind of a big deal about zero tolerance. Drugs being the number one problem in Mason County. I don't need to tell you that."

"It was in the glove box of a borrowed vehicle," she said. "It belonged to the dad. They didn't even know it was there." She could hear herself, her voice rising. She tried to get a grip. "I thought he cited them on a traffic thing."

"He did but he cited them on possession too," Theo Choate replied. "And auto theft, but that's not going anywhere." Giving her a look that said he knew what was what with Harley Rose.

"Drop it," Irene said. "Give them a break. They're good kids."

"They probably are good kids," he said mildly. "That's why I came over to see you. It always helps to know something about the family." He got up from her visitor's chair and paced across her cubicle and back, stopping to eye her photo montages. "What's this?" he said.

"Gustavus Island," she answered. "Anne Paris?" Giving it the rising inflection of a question. "It's been in the paper."

"Oh, sure," he said. "You're on that?" She nodded and he said, "What's that all about? Is that something other than an accident?"

"I don't know yet," she said. "But I think so."

He looked at her, head cocked, curious. "So?"

"I don't know," she said.

"Come on," he said, "Give me something."

"Well," she said, "there's a bunch of them out there with potential motive, and it just seems to me to be completely implausible that if it was a sailing accident she'd end up where she ended up, in the slough—you know, in an inland body of water two miles north of where the boat grounded. It just doesn't compute."

"What kind of motive?" he asked.

"The usual," Irene said.

"What's that?" he asked.

"You know, love or money, take your pick. It's not the Brady bunch out there. Or Ozzie and Harriet or whatever the apt metaphor is."

He smiled.

When the time came, if the time came, Theo Choate would evaluate the evidence she produced to support a charge, and he would either move ahead or let it drop. The department and the prosecutor worked hand in glove.

"Keeping you busy though?" he asked, looking at her keenly.

"Yeah," she said. Her tiredness had returned like a weight and she imagined it showed. She'd like to talk to someone about the case, sit down and chew it over, get some insight, think out loud, but she was already crosswise with Theo Choate, on an antagonistic footing, not collegial at all. She desperately wanted him to cut Victor some slack. As the county prosecutor he had the authority to decide which charges to pursue and which to let go. It was all his call. If she weren't so tired, she thought, she'd have played it differently, gotten on his good side somehow.

"Victor's a good boy, Mr. Choate—Theo," she said, "I don't see how prosecuting this thing is going to help. Perfectly good kids can get sort of a renegade mentality—you know, find themselves on the wrong side of the law over something inconsequential and start thinking they've got nothing left to lose."

"I know that," he said. "But perfectly good kids can also start thinking that they can get away with stuff and that the law doesn't apply to them. Sometimes some early infraction that carries consequences can sober a kid up and set him straight."

Irene wondered if he was a parent.

"What do you know about Patrick McGrath?" he asked.

"The dad's the problem there," she said. "Patrick senior. Little Patrick's okay. ADHD but they've got him taking Ritalin and it's helping."

"And the mom?"

"The mom's fine," said Irene. "I know her. She works at my dentist's office here in town, a normal, regular job."

"What's the custodial situation?"

"Joint, I think, Wednesday nights and every other weekend with the father."

"What's yours?" he asked.

Irene was caught up for a moment trying to think how to answer. A question she hadn't seen coming. "Sole," she said finally.

"Father out of the picture?"

"Out of the picture," Irene agreed. She didn't want to reveal her fragility, leave herself open to sympathy. Even after all this time she clung to Luis, hoarded him and refused to talk about him, as if he could be diminished by exposure, or she could be. She saw, though, the curious look Theo Choate threw her when she hesitated. He might have heard talk.

He walked back and forth across her office, again stopping to look at her photos. "It's a pretty spot," he said.

"Yes," she agreed.

"Whose is that giant house?" he asked.

"Guevara," she said. And she couldn't help it, she smiled and said, "Chez Guevara."

He turned and looked at her, surprised, then laughed. "Who calls it that?"

"Me and everyone else," she answered. "I don't know who thought it up."

The shared amusement altered their dynamic. "Maybe I'll meet with these kids," he said. "Have a chat."

It wasn't all she had hoped for, but it was better than it might be and she was relieved. At least he was still undecided.

"Victor have a cell phone?" he asked.

"No," she said. "You can call the house. Or swing by if you want and see if he's home. He's got a job at the corner store and he mows lawns too, you know. He works hard."

"I have no doubt," said Theo Choate.

XV

Victor wasn't yet home when Irene quit for the day. It was close to eight, the long twilight beginning to fade. She had a lot on her mind—Victor and Theo Choate and all the material she'd read during the afternoon and now had to try to assimilate. She'd go running, she decided, tired as she was. Maybe it would clear her head.

She locked her pistol into a dresser drawer, and wriggled into a jogging bra and Lycra bicycle shorts, and for modesty added the undershirt and boxers she slept in. She had good shoes she'd had fitted once when she was running regularly. She'd competed for a while, training hard and entering half-marathons and finishing high in her class. But later, when she decided to try to qualify for the Portland full marathon, she came down with a bout of bronchitis; so she'd had to lay off and had run only sporadically since.

She left a note on the kitchen table saying where she was and closed the dog inside. He wanted to go with her but he'd gotten too old and couldn't keep up. She stretched briefly on her front stoop to loosen her hamstrings, then set off down the hill, running at an easy nine-minute mile pace which she could realistically maintain for six miles, fifty-four minutes.

She crossed the railroad tracks and turned right at Lumbermen's Building Supply onto Highway 3, and ran north on the shoulder outside the fog line. In the warm evening air she could smell blackberries along the rail spur and resin and salt water as the highway rose slightly above the Simpson timber mill. Below she could see log booms laid out on the quiet water like a giant quilt, the boles of firs corralled together in a huge floating mosaic. The air was soft, fluttering her shirt around her ribs. A sheen of sweat cooled her skin. She was running easily, feeling strong.

The twilight darkened into night and overhead a thin river of stars ran between the trees. Headlights came up from behind and she glanced sideways as a pickup passed, then slowed and kept pace beside her. She checked her watch—three minutes and then she should turn around. The pickup dropped back and its lights went out, but she could still hear the rumble of the engine. A phone call, she supposed, the driver pulling over where there was a pocket of reception. All over Mason County along the two-lane highways you could see turnouts where contractors and UPS drivers and even cops, for that matter, had learned you could find cell reception. Phone booths people called them. "I'm in the phone booth up on Mason Lake Road," you might say and who-ever was asking could picture exactly where you were.

Irene wished she'd worn a headlamp or a reflective vest. Darkness had come on more quickly than she'd expected, and only the stripes on her shoes would flash her presence to an oncoming motorist. She was otherwise invisible.

Twenty-seven minutes into her run she turned around and started back. It was fully dark and she ran just to the left of the fog line, the only thing she could see to navigate by. She was still running easily, though she knew the hill home would be hard. She smelled hot metal before she saw the darker shape within the darkness, which was the pickup pulled off onto the shoulder, the engine now quiet, ticking as it cooled, and she veered onto the berm to skirt around it.

She was completely unprepared for the arm that laced out, hooking her neck and slamming her down hard onto her back, shoulder blades skidding on gravel, the wind knocked out of her and her breathing momentarily paralyzed. Someone was on top of her, pinning her arms behind her, one hand on her throat. She smelled him, smelled alcohol and sweat and cigarettes and an unwashed animal stink, and she felt his erection sliding against her midriff under her shirt as his hand yanked at her pants. Her skin was wet with sweat and the tight Lycra shorts stuck to her, resisting him.

A spectrum of survival instincts presented itself to her in a split second while she twisted beneath him. Succumb, acquiesce, said an interior voice. You will never prevail against his strength and weight. Let it happen, it will be over. Struggle is futile and dangerous. He humped against her, his weight pinning her arms.

Despite the inner voice Irene kicked and bucked, legs splayed. Then, contrary to instinct, going on the offensive, she turned her face to his and bit into the bristled skin along his jaw. Her teeth hit bone and she tasted blood. He yelled and his fist hammered into the side of her head. But he'd taken his hand from her throat and she was able to curl her body and squirm away, sliding out from under him. He grabbed at her arms but his hands slid on her wet skin and she slipped free and kicked hard, hearing him grunt as her foot connected with somewhere soft.

She ran, her breath rasping in her chest, dizzy and dazed from the blow to her head, but free. Running to save her life, running now faster than a nine-minute mile, a seven-minute mile or six-minute mile, her personal best. Behind her she heard the pickup start up, the rumble of the engine gunning away, receding. Running past Lumbermen's and up the hill as if her life depended on it, legs pumping.

On her porch two figures were silhouetted in light streaming out through the open front door. The dog, running to greet her, came up short and growled, circling her. "Hey," she whispered, and slowed to a walk, panting, trying to get her breath. The dog's muzzle like a wand at airport security running up and down her legs. He didn't like the way she smelled. "Hey," she said again softly, her hand in his fur, sorting the people on her front step into Victor and Theo Choate and walking on past, her breath whistling. They had seen her and were watching. She tasted blood in her mouth, her stomach lurched, and she dropped to her knees in the darkness on the side of the street and vomited.

"Mom," she heard Victor say.

"Go in," she called and retched again, her stomach turning inside out, thinking of his blood in her mouth and of his penis sliding against the skin under her shirt.

When the vomiting subsided, she got to her feet and went to the side of the house where the hose was coiled. She turned it on hard and sluiced her tongue and her teeth, rinsing and spitting until her mouth felt clean and cold.

Victor had gone in, but Theo Choate was still standing on her porch. She didn't want to talk, didn't want to explain, didn't want to try for normalcy or calm. She wanted to get past him, get inside, get to her gun, get her back to a wall and wait until her heart slowed and she could think. She wanted to take a shower.

As she came up the steps he moved aside. "What's wrong?" he asked as she reached for the screen door and slipped past him. She ran up the stairs and into her room and unlocked the drawer where she'd left her gun.

Walking back down the hall she heard Victor call to her from behind his bedroom door. "It's okay," she answered. "I'm okay now."

Theo Choate had followed her indoors and was standing at the bottom of the stairs when she came down with her gun in her hand. He followed her into the kitchen. She laid the gun on the table and stood at the sink with her back to him. "You're all skinned up," he said, touching her shoulder with his fingertips. Irene twitched away and yanked the cord to close the slats of the Venetian blinds in the window above the sink. She was starting to shake, a reaction setting in. She didn't want to cry. Behind her she heard him pick up the phone. "No," she said. "Don't."

"You should be seen," he said.

"No," she said again. She turned around and sat down at the kitchen table. Theo Choate winced when he saw her face.

"What happened?" he asked her again.

"Someone jumped me," she said.

"Who?"

"I didn't see him," she said. "I didn't even see the pickup to say what color it was or what make or year. But it was Patrick McGrath. Patrick McGrath Senior. The father."

"Did he—"

She knew what he was asking even though he didn't finish the question. "No," she said. "I got away."

"You should report this," he said.

"Maybe," she said, "but I'm not going to." She touched her cheekbone and eye socket gingerly.

After a moment Theo Choate said, "If you have a bag of peas you could put it on that."

"Maybe I do," she said and behind her she heard him open the freezer compartment.

"Succotash," he announced after a moment, handing it to her.

This struck Irene funny and she started to laugh but was suddenly crying after all, uncontrollable, shaky sobs. Theo Choate made a move as if to comfort her but she jerked away, wiping her cheeks with the back of her hand. "I want you to leave," she said fiercely, "I want to take a shower."

"Irene," he said, protesting. But she flashed him a steely look, and reached for the Glock where it lay on the table, meaning business. He turned to go. Irene walked down the hall behind him with the gun in her hand and locked the door as he went out.

<hr />

LATER SHE stood in the stinging hot shower for a long time, until she felt calm and clean and thought it was possible she'd sleep.

XVI

He wouldn't, Theo Choate decided as he drove away, prosecute those boys. Talking to Victor earlier he hadn't yet made up his mind. He'd knocked long and loud and it was only the dog barking that finally penetrated whatever was playing on Victor's headphones. Victor, when he appeared, was younger and less tough than the boy Theo had imagined. He looked blurry as though he might have been sleeping, but he snapped into focus when he learned who Theo was. Then he was nervous but earnest, with a solid handshake—calluses on his palm—and an engaging sidelong gaze. He offered Theo iced tea and brought it out to the porch, and they sat down side by side on the step in the gathering dusk.

Theo wondered belatedly why he'd come. Something to do with the mother perhaps, if he was honest with himself. It was arguably inappropriate for him to be here, since there wasn't anything he could legitimately ask or learn in this setting about the facts surrounding the charges.

He'd inquired generally about Victor's work, school and friends, and asked a little more pointedly about Patrick McGrath. Victor was polite and, to a lawyer's ear, admirably concise in his replies. Work was okay, he liked mowing lawns better than the grocery store, Patrick was fine. He tossed the Frisbee for the dog while they talked.

⊰◈⊱

Victor probably was a good kid, but he was at a perilous age and he'd already made at least one bad decision. Theo thought maybe he should refer the boys to Diversion, which was a citizen committee empowered to impose community service-type penalties in underage matters, in the hope of discouraging future infractions.

But leaving Irene's house—looking back through the lace panel before the light in the hall went out at the slim blonde woman in a ragged undershirt and men's boxers, a Glock semi-automatic pistol hanging by her side in one hand, a bag of frozen vegetables held against her face with the other—Theo's heart was wrenched. He thought of the alarm in Victor's voice as he'd called out to his mother, and the stricken look he'd flashed at Theo as he retreated inside. The boy and the mother seemed a fragile unit in a turbulent world, and Theo didn't think he had the stomach to become one more devil snapping at their heels. Maybe he'd see Victor and young Patrick McGrath in court some other time, but he was letting this one go. And he felt good about the decision.

⚜

Theo stopped at a hole-in-the-wall taco shop off Railroad Street and bought a plate of carnitas to go, spicy pulled pork on corn tortillas wrapped up in tinfoil with lime wedges and chopped cilantro, a smoky salsa on the side. Freddie Fender was wailing on the radio.

There was a huge Hispanic population moving north into Mason County, working the orchards and the strawberry fields and the new shellfish farms springing up along the tidelands, changing the demographic and the local culture. Theo supposed most were illegal and some probably cooked meth as well as tacos, but he liked the cuisine they brought with them and the good humor, the vivid color of their skin and clothes, their music and the shy smile of the girl who could barely understand his order. He said gracias and she said thank you and he dropped a tip that was nearly the same as the price of his meal into the jar on the counter.

Chavez, he thought walking out. Who, he wondered, was the man who had left Irene with that name and the dusky boy.

⁙

THEO DIDN'T know it, but the route he traveled in his pickup heading home was the same one Irene had run. The Shelton Yacht Club, located just past the Simpson timber mill off of Highway 3, consisted of one long dock that was home to a motley assortment of moored vessels. Theo had brought his Alaskan fishing boat south and was living aboard, modifying it in his spare time—though there was so little of that the project was in perpetual hiatus—to make it more habitable. The boat, an older wooden trawler, had nice beamy lines and relatively roomy below-deck spaces. The vessel was hooked up to water and electricity, and in these warm summer months, with a charcoal grill hanging off the deck railing and the cabin portholes and hatches open to the breeze, it was a fine place to come home to. The winter would be a different story, with mold and damp and wind and chop. But Theo was frugal and not particularly well paid and the boat had been home for many years in different seas and ports. He was content for the time being to pay moorage instead of rent while he waited to see how his new job panned out, to sleep in the vee berth up under the prow and to spread his files out over the galley table.

Theo was the only live-aboard in residence, but on Tuesday evenings and every other Saturday there were sailing regattas which brought people down to the pier, and on the weekends there was a lot of recreational boating activity and offers of drinks late in the day. Sometimes Theo crewed in the races for one neighbor or another, and he enjoyed the casual fraternity of competition and the chat about gear and rigging and strategy.

Theo had been adopted by an apparently homeless orange cat that now greeted his arrival in the parking lot and followed him down the gangway and out along the dock, attracted, Theo cynically supposed, more by the carnitas than by companionship.

Theo liked the cat and had taken to calling it Joe after a song he remembered from childhood about a marmalade cat named Joe that traveled with the rodeo. He missed it when it didn't appear and liked feeling its weight on the bedclothes in the night.

He opened a beer and sat on deck in a lawn chair in the warm dark sharing his tacos with the cat. Exploding ordnance dropped over the McChord air base lit the underbelly of the thin cloud cover rose, and the delayed booms of the concussions rolled north like thunder. Theo thought about the kids flying those planes and dropping the bombs on the practice reservation south of Tacoma, and of their mothers and their future deployments, and wondered if in a few years Victor Chavez would be one of them. There was a ceiling in Mason County and the military was one way up and out.

Theo felt unaccustomedly glum and moody. The attack on Irene Chavez upset him. He now thought that he shouldn't have been at her house in the first place, but given that he *had* been there, he shouldn't have left when he did. He should have insisted she go to the hospital or call the police, or both. He shouldn't have left her there battered and alone with only her son and her gun. She flummoxed him and he was afraid he hadn't been altogether professional. It bothered him to recognize a self-serving worm of worry that this information would come out someday and become public and embarrass him. He wondered what she was doing now.

The warm night wrapped around him, and he put his feet up on the rail and tilted back in his chair with the cat in his lap. Overhead he recognized the constellations of Orion and the Big Dipper and the W of Cassiopeia, and as he watched he could see the steady progress of a satellite or the space station floating eastward across the sky. Anywhere in this hemisphere a person looking skyward would see the same things, didn't matter if you were in Iraq or Afghanistan or Mason County, Washington, the same velvet universe enfolded you. More people should look up, Theo thought. It was humbling and unifying.

He felt a pang of missing his once wife—a woman long gone from his life—and his most recent girlfriend, a physical therapist in Sitka. Neither one had ever been truly right, but that didn't stop the empty feeling. He'd like to be getting into bed with more than a cat to wrap his arms around.

Theo wondered if he were to ask Irene Chavez out, if she'd go.

XVII

The next morning Irene started her day at the Walmart store up on the bench above town where she bought a tube of concealer and picked out a pair of enormous faux tortoiseshell sunglasses. At the register she clipped off the tag and put the glasses on. "Very Jackie O.," said the checker, sympathetically ignoring the obvious. It was dispiriting to realize the assumption of domestic violence, but convenient not to be asked to explain. Irene's eye was blue and puffy despite the icing of the night before, and she knew there would be a garish evolution before the bruising ultimately faded. She was stiff and sore and angry with herself and the world.

At the courthouse as she walked past Wanda with only a nod, the dark glasses got raised eyebrows but no comment. She decided to skip the morning meeting—with Inspector Gilbert gone it seemed optional and unnecessary. In her cubicle she didn't know where to begin. Her desk was buried in paper. She had other matters besides the Paris family to attend to which she had been neglecting. Most of it had to do with the usual—cooking, using or selling meth. A court appearance the next day on a possession with intent charge would keep her in town, but after that she thought she could shake free for a day. She eyeballed the flight schedules on her computer, then buzzed reception and asked Wanda to book a redeye to Boston and back for her. The department had a travel budget but it was rarely tapped, and she could picture Wanda's disapproval in the silence that followed the request, no doubt thinking that Irene was getting uppity in the absence of Inspector Gilbert and weighing the appropriate response. "Just do it," Irene snapped.

Next she called Officer Sean Egan, the Cambridge police officer she'd talked to previously, and left a message on his phone telling him to expect her. She would, Irene figured, either find something illuminating in Anne's Cambridge apartment or not, but she wouldn't know until she got there. She had no very clear idea of what she'd be looking for—something to help her identify the man in the Donley cabin, first of all—but she knew if she didn't investigate for herself she'd always wonder if something critical had been missed.

At the mental hospital where Anne had worked, the director's secretary didn't want to put Irene on her boss's calendar without knowing the nature of the meeting; but Irene was law enforcement and she pled confidentiality concerns and got herself squeezed in for a half an hour before lunch. Surprise was an advantage Irene always tried to retain, though in this instance she didn't expect it to yield anything of value. Still, given the option, it seemed more prudent to break the news of Anne's death in person.

⊰⊱

SITTING AT her desk Irene wrote a short list. U/K, which was her shorthand for the unknown man in the Donley cabin, her prime suspect. Ira Logan. Libby Burton. Elliot Burton. Rueben Guevara wasn't making the cut at the moment, though his apparent obsession with Anne and the feud with Dr. Paris along with the intriguing bottle of Bordeaux, held him a place on the long list.

Following Ira's name Irene wrote 'possible motive no alibi.' It was clear that Ira and Anne were having trouble and most likely breaking up. According to Ira's account he'd worked on his car until nearly dark, eaten cold leftovers standing up in the kitchen—this much was corroborated by Yvonne as near as Irene could tell with the language difficulty—then had walked down to the beach to look at the tide. The wind, he said, even then was pushing waves high up onto the dune. In the dark he hadn't thought one way or another about the presence or absence of the I-14 out on the buoy. He'd smoked a cigarette sitting on a log and had been in his cot in the barn before ten. Irene had his butt in a bag—or anyway a butt—so the part about the cigarette at the beach was corroborated. But except for the interlude in the kitchen with Yvonne, no one recalled seeing him at any point throughout the evening, though nobody seemed to think this was unusual.

Libby Burton, the same, 'possible motive no alibi.' Anne's death changed Libby's fortunes considerably just simply in terms of future inheritance. But beyond the practical matter of financial gain, always a motivator, Irene intuited an abiding resentment on Libby's part toward her younger, more favored half-sister—a less tangible but equally galvanizing factor to weigh.

Libby and the others had eaten dinner outdoors at the table on the bluff, watching the tall sail of the I-14 slice back and forth across Case Inlet in the increasing wind. The water, Libby said, turned green and whitecaps came up. It didn't occur to her to worry about her sister, she said, but her father commented anxiously to no one in particular that Anne should come in. Leland contradicted him, saying that it looked like great sailing and he wished he were out there with her.

Later Libby helped Yvonne clear the table and clean up the kitchen, and then repaired to the barn loft where she read to her boys—*Old Yeller* she said was the book, an account corroborated by Owen and Neal who wanted to know if Irene had read it and if she'd cried at the end. Irene said she had read it and, yes, she had cried, and as she answered she had to fight back tears again thinking of boys and dogs and the wrenchingness of growing up, and of reading it to Victor not that long ago.

So Libby was accounted for until she closed the book and the boys went to sleep. After that, with Elliot absent, Libby could easily have left the barn unremarked.

Elliot Burton, 'possible motive, flimsy alibi.' Elliot had flown into Burbank the day before Anne's death, rented a car and stayed with a friend in the Palisades overnight, then auditioned for a *Law and Order* spin-off at Universal Studios, returned the car and caught a flight home. There was a stop in Portland and a mechanical delay, and when the airline offered to put passengers up in a hotel or bus them to Sea-Tac, Elliot decided to rent a car and drive himself to Gustavus Island, which explained the Dodge Neon with Oregon plates. It was past midnight, he said, when he got in, and he said Libby didn't waken when he slipped in next to her. No one reported hearing or seeing him drive in in the wee hours, and he was up and out ahead of Libby and the boys, so it was really only his word as to when he'd arrived or that he'd been in bed at all. The story about the flight delay and mechanical problem was true—Irene had checked.

The unknown man. About his possible motive or alibi Irene had no idea. But he had fled. And he had broken into and been living in the Donley cabin, crimes against property that in Irene's mind made it more plausible that he'd commit crimes against persons. And he'd known Anne in some clandestine way. She would have to find him, Irene thought, though at present she didn't have the faintest idea how. She wondered if the diamond ring had come from him.

Irene's mind was going in circles. She wished she'd known Anne in life. As it was, having looked at photographs, having seen her dead body and having held her hand, Irene felt that she too had fallen a little in love with Anne Paris, under the spell of this oddly compelling, now dead, young woman. Irene felt totally committed to finding her killer and altogether stymied at the present moment.

⨳

IRENE HAD her hand on the phone when she changed her mind. She could call people in for interviews if she wished, but she decided to go out to Gustavus Island yet again. She felt like a yo-yo running up and down the string of Highway 3, but something was telling her she'd get more from them out there on their own turf. Inspector Gilbert might not agree, but he wasn't around to argue with her.

⁂

Dʀɪᴠɪɴɢ ᴏᴜᴛ of town Irene relived her run of the night before and pulled off the road where she thought it had happened. She thought she saw scuff marks in the gravel shoulder but she wasn't certain. She felt queasy and chilled despite the summer heat.

Irene hadn't had sex with a man since Luis had died, eleven years ago. She'd never dated, not because of any sort of principle or promise or prohibition, she just hadn't been interested. She'd worked and looked after Victor, and it had seemed like enough. She had rebuffed offers and interest, building a wall that most men recognized and didn't even try to penetrate. But the sheer weight of elapsed time lent import to her abstinence. It was almost like being a virgin again, a state she wouldn't change lightly. Last night had nearly ended that.

Standing there in the warm August morning she realized that Theo Choate had been right the night before, she should have made a report, should have been seen at the hospital. Her head hurt and she ached all over. When she got back from Gustavus, she decided, she'd make a belated record of what had happened. One of the other deputies could go out to Patrick McGrath's trailer and talk to him, look for a laceration on the side of his jaw and bring him in if there was one. In her imagination she tasted his blood in her mouth again. She wondered if she should have some sort of test.

XVIII

Ira Logan was lying on his cot with a road map open against his knees when Irene walked into the barn. "Hey," she said.

"Hey," he said back, clicking off the headlamp he was using to read.

Irene circled the Triumph, inspecting it. It looked finished, all the dials and gauges fitted into a gleaming walnut dashboard, no more dangling wires, no tools littering the floorboards.

Ira folded up the map and hitched himself into a sitting position, making room for her at the foot of the cot, but she sat down on an upended five-gallon bucket nearby and looked at the collection of items stored behind him on the crosspiece in the stud wall. A prescription vial was one thing. She wondered what it held. It was dim in the barn, she couldn't see very well, and she'd like a closer look. A half-empty bottle of Maker's Mark, a thick paperback copy of a Swedish mystery everyone was reading, and an oyster shell he'd been using for an ashtray.

"You're back," he said.

"I am," she replied. "Got to wrap this thing up."

"Cool," he said. Then, "What's with the shades?"

Irene flipped the dark glasses up onto her forehead, looking steadily at him. Ira snapped his headlamp back on and leaned in close, blinding her. Her eyes blinked closed and she felt him touching her cheekbone and eye socket, moving the tips of his fingers firmly but gently in a little pattering palpation pattern around the area of damage.

"Ouch," he said, leaning back. "What happened?"

Irene didn't answer. She opened her eyes and slid the glasses back into place. End of discussion.

He shrugged as though he didn't care, but she could tell he was piqued. He had wanted to be let into her confidence.

"Have you been seen?" he asked.

"No."

"Any nausea, anything like that?"

"No," she said, "I'm fine."

"Yeah," he said, "you probably are. Responsive pupils, no apparent fractures. But that's a doozy. You should probably have an x-ray."

Looking at her that way, touching her clinically, he'd turned her into a patient, and turned the tables, reminding her of his status and education and of her own vulnerability. She thought for a moment of his professional life in the emergency room, seeing all the horrible stuff that happens to people. Maybe, she thought, it hardened a person. Maybe Ira, who saved lives, felt entitled to take one. She wondered.

"Ira," she said, "Anne was seeing someone—who?"

"What do you mean Anne was seeing someone?" he asked. He looked genuinely puzzled.

"She wasn't?" asked Irene.

"Seeing someone like a shrink you mean?"

Irene laughed. 'Seeing.' She wasn't used to the nomenclature of this set. "No. Another man. Seeing another man."

"No," he said, quite emphatic, "Anne wasn't seeing anyone. Not like that."

"How do you know?"

"I just know." he said. "I mean, she was unhappy, I told you that, about the girl in Ecuador that *I* saw. Well, saw is the wrong word. You know what I mean. My fandango or whatever you call it. She was pissed, that's for sure. But seeing someone, no."

"Were you engaged?"

"Engaged?" he said.

"Had you bought her a ring?" asked Irene.

"No," he said. "You mean like go pick out a rock and present it on bended knee?"

"Yeah, more or less."

"I don't think guys do that these days," he said. "But we had an understanding."

"There's a really big diamond from Tiffany's among her things," said Irene.

Ira gave her a long, thoughtful look. "No kidding," he finally said.

"No kidding," she said. There was a silence.

"Maybe it was her mother's."

"Not according to Dr. Paris."

"She never wore it," he said.

"So where'd it come from?" asked Irene.

"How would I know where it came from?" he snapped, "I never saw anything like that. Things weren't that great at the moment but I'd have known if there was someone else. I mean, you'd know something like that." He sounded, she thought, the tiniest bit insecure. Maybe he was telling the truth.

"I think you did know," she said, pushing.

Ira's face hardened. "What's that supposed to mean?"

"Exactly that. I think you did know. I think it was over between you. I think that *that* was your understanding. Finish fixing your car and clear out. And I don't think you were happy about it."

"I *am* finished," he said. "And I'm out of here, you're right about that part."

"Oh?" she said, "When?"

"Tomorrow. I'm going home. And you can't stop me unless you arrest me and you're not going to do that. You're fishing, that's all. You don't know *what* happened to Anne, how she died or anything."

"How long is this transcontinental expedition going to take?" Irene asked.

"It'll take however long I feel like taking," he said. "I'm going to head east and take the Hi-line across Montana and cut up into

Canada. It'll take a while. Six days maybe. Eight days. Maybe more. I don't know."

"Answer your phone and check your messages," said Irene, "and let me know if you're broken down somewhere. You've got my card."

"You bet, Detective. Wouldn't want to lose touch." His voice was bitter, none of the easy flirtatiousness of before. She'd made him very angry.

Irene wondered if it was wise to let him go, knowing he'd be out of the country in Canada for part of his journey—it wouldn't be easy to extract him from there if she decided she needed to. Oh, well, she thought, he was right, of course. To keep him here she'd have to charge him with something and she had nothing. She didn't really believe that he'd killed Anne—though the flash of anger was interesting and unexpected—just that he had a possible motive and no real alibi.

XIX

E lliot Burton, Irene thought, was nervous as a cat and she wondered why. They were sitting in the Adirondack chairs in front of the Paris house near the bluff and he kept shifting position as though he couldn't get comfortable. He was handsome in a slightly blurred, boyish way. He kept running his fingers through abundant wavy auburn hair, raking it back off a high, pale forehead.

"I can't believe this," he said. "I'm just having a really hard time with it. I wish I'd been here. I don't know, I just feel totally weird."

The 'everything happens to me' sort, thought Irene. A person who, no matter what happens or to whom, it's always *their* story.

"How are your boys doing, do you think?" she asked.

"The boys," he said, "Yeah. They seem okay."

"And your wife?"

"Oh, Libby's fine."

"How come it's so hard for you?" Irene asked.

He swiveled his head and gave her a baffled look. "Well," he said, "it's hard on everybody actually. Nobody's fine. I didn't mean *that*."

Irene waited. People like Elliot talked, they filled silences. She'd learned that over the years.

"Nobody's fine," he said again. "I mean, Libby's not fine, she's *coping* is what I meant. You know, I'm sure you've noticed, she's just furiously mowing all the time. This is a totally weird family. No one ever says how they feel. Everyone just goes around with a long face looking somber and holding it all in. No one talks about it. No one cries even. Have you noticed that?" he asked, turning to look at her. "No one cries."

"Maybe no one's sad," said Irene.

"Well, Oliver's sad," he replied, "that's for sure." Then quickly, "I'm sad. We're all sad. It's just such a shock it's hard to know *how* you feel."

"What was your relationship with Anne?" Irene asked.

"My relationship," he said, "what do you mean? Brother-in-law."

"Did you like her? How did you get along?"

"Oh, that," he said. "Well, we were close actually," his voice softening. "I mean, we always had a special bond. I don't know why really, but we did." Elliot, defying the Paris family reticence, choked up. He flushed and put a hand to his face, pinching the corners of his eyes as tears leaked down his cheeks. Irene watched. It could, she thought, be a performance, but it looked like real grief.

"How close?" asked Irene. "Did you sleep with her?" She didn't know why she asked it, the question just popped into her head.

Elliot turned and looked at her, speechless. He wagged his head slowly, more in wonderment than denial, as though such an outlandish concept took a lot of getting used to. It was a long moment before he echoed, "Sleep with her? I'd never do that. I could never do that to Libby."

But Irene wondered. She thought it was possible he could look right at her and lie. An innocent lamb. It was what he was trained to do, his profession, make faking look real. She was amazed by a sudden welling frustration. She felt like slapping him. "Did you get the part?" she asked.

"What?" he said.

"In L.A., the television part."

"Oh," he said, "I don't know, I haven't heard." He brightened, "It went well." He looked at his watch. "I should call," he said, "call my agent." He paused, then went on. "They never want you to call. They hate for you to call, but the waiting sucks. You know, always waiting for the phone to ring. Bad news travels fast, they say, but in this business it's the opposite. You get the part and they're on the phone before you're even home from the audition. They act like they got it for you, hallelujah—you're great, they're great, love, peace, and brown rice. You *don't* get it, they wait two weeks to let you know and that whole time you're still halfway hoping. You know better, but even so, you still hope. We could use the money," he added glumly.

"What was Libby's relationship with her like?"

"With Anne?"

"Yes, with Anne." Deliberately changing the subject, trying to keep him off-balance.

"Oh, well," he said after a minute. "It's just like happenstance really that Libby's even part of this family. Libby's entire life experience is completely different. Moving back to Texas, teacher's daughter, hardscrabble. It's hard for me to think of them as sisters even."

"That doesn't answer my question," said Irene.

"No," he said. "But, you know, in fact Anne adored Libby. She admired her."

"How do you know that?" asked Irene.

"I know because she told me," he said. "But you could tell. To Anne, Libby was exotic. Libby's such a cowboy and Anne admired that. Anne liked to borrow her clothes, dress up like her. Her Levi jacket, her snappy shirts, hooded sweatshirt. Stuff like that. Libby's authentic in a pretty amazing way. She's tough."

He drifted off in his own thoughts. It took a moment before he turned back to her. "She was born with teeth, Libby was, the sign of a witch. Her mother told me that. But all Libby sees is what she never had and won't ever have. The Barnard education, all the pretty dresses, money, Daddy. She's bitter, if you want to know the truth. It's all about Oliver really, when it comes down to it. For Oliver, the sun rose and set on Anne. Libby could never get his attention."

Pretty much what Irene had thought.

"Do you smoke?" he asked.

"No," said Irene.

"Hardly anyone does anymore. In L.A. they still smoke." He flashed her a smile. "Do you want a beer?" He was levering himself out of his chair. "I want a beer."

In a moment he was back, sliding in beside her again with two frosty IPAs hooked between his fingers, offering her one. She did want a beer but she shook her head no and watched as he twisted off the cap and tipped it back. He *was* nervous, Irene thought, needing the beer more than just wanting it. Calming his nerves.

"Where is everyone?" she asked.

"I don't know," he said. "We're all a little catatonic. Oliver is in his study. At least I assume he's in his study. He always is. Nikki and Rosie are doing Pilates. It's their big summer activity, the three of them—well, obviously not the three of them now. The two of them. Every morning they watch a DVD on Anne's computer and follow along. Abdominal exercises for core strength."

"Right," said Irene, peeved. She didn't need Pilates defined. She wasn't that provincial. "We're actually in possession of Anne's computer at the moment," she said, thinking that was something else she needed to follow up on. Someone was supposed to be working on getting past Anne's passwords and deeper into her files and documents and internet history.

"That makes sense," he said. "I guess Nikki's got a computer because they're inside watching the Pilates DVD. I just saw them. And Libby," he went on, "I don't know. I think she's in the orchard pruning. These old apple trees, they're heirloom apples and they've been neglected so long it's hard to know what to do. She's not mowing or we'd hear the machine. Ira," he said, "presumably is in the barn. At least that's where he was earlier when I came down from the loft. He hasn't exactly resurfaced after all this. He was just lying on his cot." He caught himself and looked sharply at her. "You did know he's been—well, I'm sure you did know he's been sleeping in the barn."

Irene nodded yes.

"Yvonne's been carrying his meals out to him," Elliot continued. "She likes him because he understands French. He gets special dispensation. And Leland walked down the beach to Nigel's with my boys, looking for a drink. That's where I was headed when you showed up. Is that everybody?" he asked, ticking off on his fingers.

Looking for a drink, Irene thought. It wasn't even noon. "What are you going to do with your rental car?" she asked.

He looked at her. "Yeah," he said, "that's a problem I didn't really think about at the time. They really hammer you on these one-way rentals."

"What was your big hurry?" she asked.

"No big hurry," he said.

"Why didn't you sit it out in Portland?"

He thought for a minute. "I was thinking I got the part, to tell you the truth, feeling flush. Feeling good about things. I was up, you know. Upbeat. Sitting around or taking a bus seemed lame, a loser deal. I've been there. It saps you, grinds you down. Being an actor, you have no control over how your life goes. It's always someone else's call." He glanced at her. "You probably can't imagine the difference between getting the part and not getting the part. It isn't just the money. The money's big, don't get me wrong, but it's more than that. It's psychological. It's affirmation. You're good. What you do matters. They treat you like royalty, fly you first class. Everyone makes a fuss. I rented a Neon, as you may have noticed. I'd rather have rented a luxury car or a specialty car. I'd like to try out the Solara or the Cayenne or something fun. God, a Taurus even."

"You weren't in a hurry to get home?"

He looked at her. "I was in a hurry to get home in the ordinary sense of wanting to get home instead of spending a night on a stinking bus or in some lame airport hotel." He was getting increasingly worked up. "Obviously it was a bad idea. Now I'm stuck with a rental car I don't quite know how to unload and my own car is parked up at Sea-Tac racking up a tab, my wife is furious and this situation down here makes it a little harder to take off again to deal with any of it. Plus, now here *you* are, trying to make something out of it." He looked at his watch again.

"I need to call. This whole thing sucks. The business sucks. If you'd asked me yesterday I'd have said I had the part. This was a good part. It was recurring. I'd have been a regular. I needed it." He got up.

Elliot, Irene thought, had money troubles. Money troubles and a troubled conscience. Her phone was vibrating on her belt and she nodded up at him, reaching for the phone, dismissing him, the interview over.

It was Victor—Victor who never called—stabbing her with anxiety.

"Hi, honey," she said, walking toward her car, trying to keep the worry out of her voice, "what's up?" Victor had been asleep when she left the house.

"Nothing," he said, "just checking. Are you at work?"

"I am," she said. "What about you?"

"I'm going to work," he said. "I'm off at seven."

"I'll be home," she said.

⟶⟨⟩⟵

AND SHE was. She stopped for groceries and was home earlier than she'd been in weeks. She grilled a chicken breast, shredded it and tossed it together with chopped romaine and a dressing she made with lemon, garlic and an egg. Something lean and green after weeks of drive-through.

"What happened, Ma?" Victor asked.

She glanced up. He wasn't looking at her. They'd eaten the salad at the table in the backyard, talking of other things. There was a bicycle Victor wanted with a fixed gear, something she didn't quite understand and he tried to explain—more retro than anything, he said, an old school bike with only one gear and no brakes. To stop you stood on the pedals. She thought it sounded dangerous but Victor said no, not once you got used to it. He'd seen a used one advertised in the Olympia paper and thought he might buy it. He had enough money. He wondered if she could drive him down there to try it out, and she said yes, on her next

⁓ 130 ⁕

day off. But when he asked when that would be she couldn't answer. After her trip to Boston she guessed.

Then they were silent for a while until he asked, "What happened, Ma?" not looking at her. Something in his voice telling her that he was afraid for her safety and afraid that whatever happened had something to do with him; that there was something he should do about it but he wasn't sure what or that he was up to doing it. He wasn't a child anymore, but the child he'd been didn't want to lose another parent to violence, and he wasn't yet sure how to be the man he was becoming or what was required of him.

Minimize it, she thought. He doesn't want details, he wants reassurance. "It was something to do with work and it's taken care of," she said. "I filed a report and it's handled." Which was true. She'd come back into town and written up an account and handed it in to the chief deputy, making a record. "I'm fine," she said.

"Okay," Victor said.

And that was that. He'd wanted reassurance and she'd given him enough to let him believe that the grown-ups were handling it, other people knew, and he could go back to being a kid. But she'd seen, had a glimpse anyway, of his very adult awareness that it was a perilous world out there where things you didn't see coming could change your life in an instant.

Now she was wondering what had passed between Theo Choate and Victor the night before. She hadn't thought about it at the time, but looking back it seemed obvious that Theo had done as she suggested and stopped by the house, and had probably come to some determination about what he was going to do about Victor and Patrick. Then she turned her mind away. The evening was warm and pleasant, she was glad to be home, and she didn't want to think about the night before.

Victor got up and took the plates in without being asked. In the street out front Irene heard the approach of an ice cream truck—a sound of summer—and after a while Victor came back around the house eating an Eskimo Pie with one for her. For the first time in a long time Irene felt totally content and in the moment.

XX

Theo Choate had seen Irene's name on the witness list for the day's calendar, so he wasn't surprised when she slipped into the courtroom at the start of the afternoon calendar; but as soon as she appeared he felt himself divided, as though one Theo Choate, the prosecutor, went about his day's business as usual, while another Theo Choate watched critically from someplace outside his person and kept up a running commentary on his diction, grooming, grammar, necktie, inducing a crippling self-consciousness.

Irene, on the other hand, wearing dark glasses, narrow black trousers, a snug black jacket, and pumps that made her taller than he remembered as she walked past him when she was called, seemed completely composed and professional. There was nothing in her manner or her expression or the direction of her gaze to indicate they'd ever met or that she had the slightest interest in him.

She took the stand without removing the glasses, but took them off to be sworn. She looked better than he would have expected—the puffiness around her eye had subsided and whatever bruising had developed was mostly hidden under a thick plaster of makeup. If you didn't know to look for it you might not even notice.

The questioning and her testimony was perfunctory, just the dry recounting of the facts surrounding the investigation that had led up to a raid in the woods off Benson Lake Road, where a couple of entrepreneurs were cooking meth in a seventeen-foot travel trailer surrounded by chain-link fencing that contained a vigilant and angry pit bull. Irene related the demeanor of the accused during the arrest and the evidence that had been collected at the scene. Theo needed the testimony and he was glad she'd appeared. Sometimes officers didn't show up, too busy or unwilling to give up time off, and then it was always harder to get a conviction.

When she left the stand, Theo thought she slid her eyes in his direction in the instant before she replaced the sunglasses.

XXI

Shortly after midnight Jet Blue Flight 67 took off to the south, looping westward over Case Inlet and Gustavus Island before banking into a lazy eastward turn and climbing above the lights of Tacoma. Even at this hour Interstate 5 was a river of light. It was odd, Irene thought looking down, how things resembled other things—the highway seen from above at night looking like corpuscles in a vein viewed under a microscope in some long ago biology film. And continuing the line of thought, cars looked like animals—how would an alien know the difference—headlights for eyes and mirrors for ears and grills and bumpers for noses and mouths. And animate too, darting here and there, stopping and starting. She wondered if anyone else had thought about it, written a dissertation.

Passing close over the luminous shoulder of Mount Rainier as the plane climbed to its cruising altitude, Irene thought of the mountaineers below, dozens of them, scores maybe, waking now in their tents, preparing for their ascent. She imagined the cold and the anticipation. Not everyone who tried made it and some never came back. The mountain, which loomed so large over Puget Sound and looked so serene from a distance, stood more than fourteen thousand feet and was not benign at all. Every year lives were lost. Irene thought of how it looked from Gustavus, rising above the horizon, catching the sun, a halo of weather of its own creation ringing its summit.

The summer after high school graduation Nigel Strauss had climbed Mount Rainier. Irene's mother had sent a clipping from the *Mason County Journal* with a note jotted in the margin to the effect of what a waste of time, exclamation point. It was a class thing. Irene's family worked physically hard for a living and at the end of the day collapsed onto the sofa. A game of horseshoes in the backyard once in a while was Irene's father's most taxing recreation. He'd scoffed at Irene's running. She couldn't quite get her mind around why this was so. Just tired, she supposed, and resentful of anyone whose job left them with enough oomph left over to turn physical exertion from a grinding necessity into something recreational and pleasurable.

Irene inclined her head and closed her eyes as the terrain below became distant and indistinct before vanishing beneath a high cloud cover. She slept.

⟨⟨⟩⟩

THE ATKINS Psychiatric Hospital was a collection of red brick buildings strewn across ten rolling, iron-fenced acres in Belmont, a little northeast of Boston. Stately maples and elms lined the drive leading from the entryway gates to an open quadrangle. It might be a college or a prep school, except that some of the windows were barred. Irene pulled her rental car into a visitor's spot in front of a Federalist-style administration building. It was shortly before ten but already hot, the mercury and the humidity both in the nineties. Irene wondered how people here managed. As soon as she stepped out of the car she was limp and filmed with perspiration, her tee shirt sticking to her.

She had flown all night, sleeping only fitfully, was tired, and wished for a shower. She felt squashed, as though gravity here were stronger, the weight of all that moisture in the air pressing down. It was hard to catch her breath. She'd brushed her teeth in the ladies' room at Logan and dabbed around her eye with the concealer stick, before picking up her car and navigating through the tunnels and intricacies created by the infamous Big Dig. The rental car was equipped with a GPS, and she had entered her destination into the navigation system, turning left and right as the robotic voice instructed. She was glad for the assistance. The streets were narrow and congested and traffic traveled at breakneck speed. Whizzing along Storrow Drive paralleling the Charles, she glimpsed arched bridges crossing the river, like pictures of Paris, and passing Back Bay, tall houses with verdigris roofs. Irene had never been east before and she felt as though she was in Europe, somewhere foreign and exotic, somewhere with a long history, more settled and solemn than the boisterous, outlaw west she called home. There was a moist dazzle in the air, haloing objects. She had the air-conditioning cranked up and the windows closed.

Here at Atkins she had a little window of time in which to interview the director, Anne's clinical supervisor, before meeting Officer Sean Egan at the Cambridge apartment.

She got out, wrestled herself into a black linen jacket, covering the gun under her arm, and ran her fingers through her hair. Indoors surely it would be air-conditioned.

The entry door was locked and she announced herself over an intercom—Detective Irene Chavez from Washington State here to see the medical director, Dr. Storey Lindstrom. After what seemed like a long wait, a receptionist appeared and let her in. She was asked to sign in and wait. The furniture was a mismatched assemblage of sixties Danish modern, warring with the paneled walls and mullioned windows dating from the Colonial era.

Dr. Lindstrom, when he appeared, was tall and rangy, gaunt even, a little hollow in the chest with narrow shoulders and a slightly oversized head. But handsome. In his fifties maybe. A nice craggy face and cool blue eyes. He looked like he spent time outdoors. Irene flipped her badge for him to see, and he led her through a labyrinth of passageways and into a tall, book-lined office. He waved her into a cracked leather armchair, sat down behind a desk piled with papers, and leaned back, propping his feet on an open drawer. A window fan stirred the air and fluttered papers, but the room was not air-conditioned. Dr. Lindstrom was in his shirtsleeves.

"I'm not used to this kind of heat," Irene said.

"No one is," he said. "This is crushing. It's record-breaking. We're all dying. Most of the buildings have air-conditioning, but we're in this quaint artifact—very lovely and impractical." His smile was wry and kind and his inflection pure New York.

"You know why I'm here, I suppose," said Irene, somewhat disingenuously.

"I don't actually," he said. "You're just a name on my calendar. Somebody slotted you in but I don't know the reason why."

"Oh," she said.

"Indeed," he said, giving her a quizzical look. "I hadn't thought about it, to tell the truth. You're here from Washington State?"

"I am," she said.

"So, what is it that brings you all the way over here?"

"It's about Anne Paris."

"Anne Paris," he echoed, and she saw it register and saw a flicker of worry or concern. Surprise, the inquisitor's friend. The name, she thought, had triggered some other association and momentarily taken him somewhere else, away from her and the present moment. Something for her to pursue. But for now she had his interest. He was studying her and she thought he was deciding what to say or whether to say anything at all. Shrinks, she thought, had a way of letting their faces settle into utter neutrality. How did you learn that? Were there classes in impassivity? Did they practice in front of a mirror? When he spoke again his voice was neutral too, gently prompting in the same way she knew he'd encourage a patient to go on. "What about Anne Paris?"

"She was a doctor here?" asked Irene.

"She's a doctor here, yes," he answered. Then looking at her added sharply, "I hope that whatever it is, it's not something that's going to involve the hospital."

"And why would it?" she asked.

"I don't know," he said.

"What kind of doctor is she, Doctor?" asked Irene.

"A very talented young psychiatrist. Prominent family in the analytic world. A star, Detective Chavez. A candidate in analytic training at the Boston Institute. Very well thought of. She's on vacation at the moment—I suppose you know that—Washington State, where you're from."

Irene nodded. She could see that he was being agreeable, cooperative and informative, letting her take her time getting to the point, accustomed, she supposed, to taking the role of observer and interpreter, not needing to control or direct a conversation.

"She did her residency with us and is about to start a fellowship year. She'll continue her analytic training but focus here with us on borderlines."

"Borderlines?" Irene queried.

"Borderline personality. Very disturbed, often harm themselves. Cutters—cut themselves, maim themselves. Suicidal. It's difficult work. Young people mostly, girls primarily. She's very good, very empathic. Makes a good connection." He stopped, looking at her intently. "I'm not getting a good feeling," he said. "I think you'd better tell me what's up."

"What do you think is up, Doctor?"

"I don't know," he said.

"Something occurred to you, something crossed your mind. I saw it in your face when I said her name," said Irene.

He studied her for a moment. "It's interesting to think—to realize actually—that other professions—yours in point of fact—might have some shared capacity with our own to divine some sort of psychological truth from very subtle, ineffable physical signals. There's a study," he said, "a test, actually, that you can administer. It's easy. There are these cards, photographs of people's faces showing different expressions, and you look at them for a brief period of time—just seconds—and then say what you saw. Like anger or disgust or fear or happiness. Five or six choices. It's primitive. It's like what dogs perceive. It's there, it's just whether you see it and can interpret it, or don't see it. Essentially it comes down to is there a threat or no threat. It's something they administer to law enforcement. And law enforcement—you—they're way better than us mental health professionals at assessing peril. And the best, they're the ones who trust it, they know when to shoot and when to talk. That's what it's about, recognizing peril." He paused. "What was it you saw in my face?"

Irene smiled. "I can't tell you what I saw," she said. "Just something that makes me know that when I said 'Anne Paris' you processed something and weren't one hundred percent surprised."

"No," he said. "Maybe not. So, what's up?"

"What's up, Dr. Lindstrom, is that Anne is dead."

He gasped, stunned. It took him a moment to recover, then he said, "Oh, my." He had known that something bad was coming and he'd been braced, she had seen that, but not braced for this. Some sort of infraction or malfeasance that would be difficult or surprising or embarrassing, but dead, no. She felt brutal putting it so baldly.

"How?" he asked finally.

"It was a blow to the head," she said. "Maybe accidental, a sailing accident, a fall. We don't know yet. It's under investigation. That's why I'm here."

"Accidental," he said, "maybe accidental. That means maybe not accidental. So what, then?" When she didn't answer he said, "Foul play?"

"Right," said Irene. "Foul play can't be ruled out. Not yet. It's an unattended death."

"Fuck," he said, surprising her. He stood up, agitated, his hand to his forehead, and took a few steps behind his desk, and sat down again. "What can I do?"

"I don't know, maybe nothing. Tell me anything you can think of. Tell me why your first thought was something involving the hospital, that you hoped it wouldn't."

Storey Lindstrom sighed, leaning forward now, his elbows on the desk, face in his hands. He had let go of his impassive, neutral mask and seemed human and engaged again, collegial. "The thing about Anne, the reason I worried about her, was a concern—something I thought about as director, her supervisor, and counseled her about—that in our line of work it's important to maintain a distance. You can't get too close. It's counterproductive. It's not good for the patient and it's not good for you. You know, there's transference and countertransference of course, those are connections that we use in the analytic process. But Anne—some of it was just her personality, her style, and part of it was a theory she was developing in working with these very difficult patients, a theory that in order to help, in order to make the necessary connection with them so that they trust you, reveal themselves, open themselves to change—she blurred boundaries. She let them believe that in some future way she might figure in their lives. It's very audacious, very controversial.

"In therapy we have what's called the 'frame,' a safe place within which the therapy is carried on. Within the frame it's safe to say anything, feel anything. That's why it's so hard for people to encounter their therapists in everyday situations—at the symphony or the grocery store. Outside of the frame there is no frame of reference, so to speak, no guidelines for the relationship." He smiled. "Anne didn't rule out some future personal connection. She let patients have her home phone number, her cell phone number. She made herself available. Let them believe in their importance to her outside the frame, beyond the therapeutic relationship. 'Allow them room for hope,' she'd say, 'don't close the door on anything.' Normally, you know, success in analysis or psychotherapy is measured by arriving at a point of not needing the analyst anymore. Anne's boundaries weren't always clear. I thought she might be vulnerable, that a patient or the parent of a patient—if something went wrong she could be open to an accusation, an ethics charge, a lawsuit. We all are, frankly. This is not an exact science and we're working with very troubled people."

He paused and looked at Irene. "I want to be very clear. There never was an ethics charge. Never. She was very passionate about what she was doing and she knew the risks, she knew that not everyone endorsed her methods or her theories. But she got results. The results are compelling. She helped people."

"When you say ethics, Doctor, sex with a patient?"

He gave her a long, tired look. "It's more complicated than that. It's the promise or hope of sex, the hope of love, of a connection beyond the therapeutic dynamic—something more than the necessity of eventual termination. But, Detective Chavez, there was never a charge. I'm simply answering your question. She was a very engaged clinician."

"Is there a particular instance, a particular patient, you're thinking of?" Irene asked.

"A particular patient," he said. "No, no particular patient."

She held his eye. "Who?"

He gave her an affectless gaze, impassive, opaque.

"I need to see her files," said Irene, "patient records, her notes, calendars."

"HIPAA protects all of that," he replied. "You'll need a court order."

"I'll get a warrant," said Irene.

"If you must," he said.

She waited.

"There's a patient," he said finally, "a patient of Anne's, someone she's treating here at Atkins, but not a legally committed patient, not someone we have legal responsibility for, but here for voluntary inpatient treatment. A case I'm supervising. August is always hard. Patients hate it when their doctors go on vacation. This particular patient, a difficult, very troubled patient, was extremely unhappy about Anne's absence, and left."

"Left?" asked Irene.

"Walked out. There's been no contact with the family, none with us here at the hospital. It's a worry. It isn't surprising. Actually it's not uncommon. Unless they're committed, we can't keep them. Usually they discharge themselves—against medical advice. This one just disappeared. It's August, the therapist is on vacation, they feel abandoned, resentful. Anyway, if you saw something, some worry or concern, that's what you saw—a patient we haven't heard from. That's all.

"Man or woman?" asked Irene.

"Oh," said Dr. Lindstrom, "a man."

Irene's heart rate ticked up. She wished she had a photo of the stranger on the beach—his face so clear in her mind's eye she felt it ought to be possible to transfer it directly into Dr. Lindstrom's brain. "What does he look like?" she asked. "Is there a photo?"

"A photo," said Dr. Lindstrom. "No, I don't think there's a photo. Maybe. I don't quite know all the intricacies of the intake procedure. We could find out. Late twenties, I'd say. Mid-twenties. Dutch descent. Kind of Slavic bone structure. Fair. Nice looking."

Momentary disappointment, then Irene moved on. Too bad. It wasn't her stranger, which, if it had been, would have tied things up nicely. Nothing was that easy.

"I've been out there, you know," said Dr. Lindstrom after a moment, "to their place on that island. Twice. Two different summers. I can picture it exactly. Berry picking. Hunting in the woods for wild mushrooms. The beach in the afternoon. Swimming with the seals in that frigid water. Meals on the lip of the cliff."

Irene smiled, picturing it herself.

"Anne loved it and she was different there. Relaxed. She was at home." He paused. "How is the family?"

"Pretty much as you'd expect, I guess," said Irene.

"So sad for Oliver," he said. "So soon after Julia. How does he seem?"

"Devastated."

"Devastated," he echoed. "Losing Julia was hard. I went out to San Francisco for the memorial. But losing Anne—I can't imagine Oliver without Anne. She was his golden child. His darling girl. The sun rose and set on Anne. She hung the moon. It wasn't a secret. He wrote about it. She wrote about it."

"Wrote about what? What wasn't a secret?" Irene asked.

"Their relationship. The erotized nature of their relationship."

"What does that mean, erotized?"

A quick apologetic smile, but he'd used the word on purpose to probe for the edge of her knowledge and vocabulary. "It's from erotic, of course, meaning he perceived her sexually, not just paternally. And vice versa too. It's a little out of the ordinary. In a different sort of family it can lead to incest, abuse."

"She was a sexual lightning rod, wasn't she?" said Irene after a moment.

"You could say that," he said.

"For you too?" she asked.

He shot her a quick look. "No," he said, "not for me. Well, maybe at one time. Early on. But it's the way she interacted with the world. Whether you went down that road with her or not, it was her half of any duet. Always very seductive, very intimate—sharing a secret with you. Very certain of her welcome in the world." He looked very intently at Irene. "You wouldn't be here if you thought it was an accident."

"No," she said, "you're right. It's my feeling—and this isn't based on anything in particular, it's just my gut—but I don't think she fell or was whacked on the back of the head by the boom of a sailboat. She was found in the slough—do you remember the slough there at the bottom of the orchard?—miles from where her sailboat grounded. She had boyfriend troubles to say the least. She was, I believe, sleeping with at least one other man besides the boyfriend. She has troubled and angry siblings—a furious sister. No, I don't think it was an accident." Sounding more vehement than she intended.

Dr. Lindstrom was silent for a long moment. "As law enforcement," he said finally, "it must be very hard when you deal with people whose values are not your own."

"I deal with people all the time whose values are not my own," snapped Irene. "It's nothing to do with values. Nothing. It's dangerous behavior, that's all. Come on, you know why crimes are committed as well as I do. Greed, jealousy, fear of exposure."

"Has it been in the papers?" he asked.

"A notice in the *Mason County Journal*," Irene said. "Summer resident, apparent boating accident."

"How come you're such a terrier on this? Why not let it go?"

It was a question she hadn't seen coming, a question she was unprepared to answer. But she thought about it for only a moment, then said, "Why would I let it go? I'm a cop, Dr. Lindstrom, it's my job."

"Hmm," he murmured, lifted eyebrows indicating his skepticism.

"I saw her," said Irene, "I saw her dead body. I held her hand. She was a smart girl and a pretty girl, an accomplished person in the midst of her life. She didn't need to die. I want to know who did this."

<hr/>

Back in the car, Irene was grateful for the air-conditioning. She didn't quite know how it had gone with Dr. Lindstrom. She knew more now, she'd learned some things, but he was cagy, opaque, and protective of the hospital. She wondered if she could have pressed harder, if there'd been an advantage she didn't gain. You didn't get do-overs with this kind of interview. You had your shot and showed your cards. Surprise was only on your side once. He would be circling the wagons now, directing staff not to talk, monitoring communications. There was something, she thought, that was elusive and important, something about Anne as a person, as a therapist—her personality and her availability—that made her vulnerability more plausible. No one was neutral on the subject of Anne. She wondered if she would have done better if she weren't tired, if she hadn't flown all night, if it were cooler. She wondered if she was out of her league. She was dealing with smart, educated, psychologically sophisticated people. She felt blunt and provincial in comparison.

XXII

Trees totally unlike the familiar, brooding conifers of home lined Fresh Pond Drive and shielded Longfellow's yellow clapboard house on Brattle. At a corner market where Irene stopped for coffee and a doughnut, the clerk's accent was startling—a's flat as Kennedy's. She felt again like Alice or Dorothy, traveling in a different universe.

The house was on Huron Street, a three-story frame structure painted barn red, porches across the front at each level, the roots of a copper beech in the front yard lifting the sidewalk—a house like all its neighbors in this part of Cambridge, tall, gawky, almost rickety. There must have been a building trend at some point in the last century. The houses were all too large for the lots, shoulder to shoulder, leaving narrow side yards used for off-street parking and garbage cans. Irene pulled up behind the black-and-white parked in front.

Officer Sean Egan was younger than she had expected, with black Irish good looks, dark hair, fair skin, weirdly pale hazel eyes—and a boxer's pitched forward, balanced stance. He looked her over as they shook hands, noting, she thought, though he didn't comment, her discolored eye, the concealing makeup atomizing in the heat and humidity. "Landlord's not here, boss," he said, "but on his way. I can let you in."

Boss. She wondered if he said it ironically, tweaking her—rural heat from the sticks, not to be taken seriously, messing with his day.

The house would once have been a single-family dwelling, now converted to a duplex, with the landlord occupying the bottom two floors and Anne's apartment on top. The foyer was more elegant than the exterior would have suggested, with a black and white marble floor, paneled pocket doors leading presumably into the landlord's living space opposite the stairs, and a kitchen entrance straight ahead—a window in the door giving a glimpse of tall, glass-fronted cabinets. There was a Persian miniature in a gilt frame on the wall, which, when Irene leaned in to look more closely, she realized was erotic—a delicately painted vignette showing a prince or king in some sort of glade or garden, his hands on the hips of a courtesan kneeling before him, his enormous penis about to enter her, while attendants with averted faces awaited in surrounding thickets. For a moment Irene was transported—then she looked away in confusion, embarrassed and aroused.

A trench coat, a Panama hat, and a Red Sox baseball cap hung on an antique hall tree, and Irene glimpsed her own hot and disheveled face in the beveled mirror next to Sean Egan's amused, pale visage. In the mirror he smiled. He had been there before and knew what she had seen.

A road bike leaned against the stairs beside a blue and white Chinese porcelain umbrella stand. This, Irene thought, was where Anne came home every night, to a cool marble hall and a bit of highbrow pornography. She was interested now in meeting the landlord, Dr. Bernstein, who, she had learned, was an organic chemistry professor at Barnard. She wondered if the bicycle belonged to Ira or to him.

Irene followed Sean Egan up two flights of steep, worn wooden stairs, too narrow to meet modern building codes, and arrived at a landing on the top level in front of the locked and sealed door to Anne's apartment. They were both huffing slightly with the exertion. Two flights below Irene heard the front door open and a man's voice called, "Hello?"

"Officer Egan, sir," shouted Officer Egan, "Cambridge PD."

"Right," came the voice, "let yourself in. I'll be up in a moment."

Officer Egan cut the seal and unlocked the door, standing back to let Irene enter. Here, on the third story, the east-facing windows were capturing the late morning sun filtering through the coppery leaves of the beech outside, and the room was suffused in rosy light and was hot as an oven. Officer Egan moved quickly to shove wide the French doors that opened onto the porch. Irene looked around. They had stepped directly into Anne's living room, a long narrow room running across the front of the house under sloping eaves. It was a pretty and comfortable room—white sofa, worn Oriental rug on the dark plank floor, a wooden trunk for a coffee table, book-lined walls, a dining table against the back wall, one end piled with catalogues and magazines. Irene could see the kitchen, white and old-fashioned, beyond a short cupboard-lined butler's pantry. On the other end of the room a similar passage led past a bathroom to the bedroom. Start in the bedroom, she decided, in the back of the apartment, and work forward. It wouldn't take long.

Shrinks had a penchant for mid-century Danish furniture. She wondered why that was. The Oriental rugs she understood—Freud's room had had one, she'd seen pictures—but Danish modern hadn't yet been invented in Freud's time. On a leggy, two-drawer teakwood nightstand there was a framed photo of Anne and Ira in happier days in a sailboat somewhere, shoulder to shoulder, leaning into each other, backs against the gunwale. She searched quickly through the drawers. This was routine for her, something she was trained in. People's personal lives revealed themselves, but it was more than that you were searching for, it was something unexpected, the item that didn't fit—like the elementary school exercise, hat, coat, scarf, banana, boots, circle one.

Out in the other room she heard Officer Egan greet the landlord and the landlord's voice responding. She was moving quickly, on to the closet now—clothes jammed together, exploding off the hanging rod above shoes, shoe boxes, shopping bags. In the full-length mirror fastened to the inside of the closet door she glimpsed the room reflected behind her, the living room beyond, and the man moving through the doorway toward her.

Her heart stopped and her breath caught, she was reaching for the gun under her arm, sinking into a crouch, before she even began to pivot. One knee on the closet floor, arms together, outstretched, right hand supporting the left, the pistol steady as Gibraltar and pointed at his chest, arresting his forward momentum—his hands lifting, palms out in shock and fear, eyes on the gun, peril registering before recognition. Then his gaze lifted and he looked at her face, recognition dawning as they stared at each other. The landlord, Dr. Bernstein, was the man in her binoculars on the beach, the face in the speeding car.

Behind him Officer Egan's startled face appeared in the doorway, taking in the tableau.

"Who *are* you?" breathed Julian Bernstein. Then, his eyes flickering to Officer Egan, "Who *is* she?" Fear and alarm in his voice. "What's *she* doing here?"

"Detective Irene Chavez," said Officer Egan blandly, "from Washington State. As arranged." Mildly, "You two know each other?"

"Cuff him," said Irene.

"Easy, boss," said Egan.

"Detective Chavez," repeated Dr. Bernstein, processing.

"Right," she snapped.

"I talked to you," he said.

"Right," she said again.

"I didn't know it was *you*," he said.

"Now you do," she said. She thought about the times he'd seen her—walking barefoot on the beach in her plainclothes and later whizzing past in her unmarked car. Nothing to suggest an officer of the law. Her name, her voice on the phone, not connected to any image of her. No wonder he was surprised. As much a surprise to him as to her. They had no more expected each other than the man in the moon, though she'd been seeking him while he'd probably never imagined he'd see her again. Her heart was slowing. She straightened up out of her crouch, keeping the gun trained on him. "Cuff him," she said again, "We're taking him in."

Officer Egan rolled his eyes but she jerked her chin and he made a little pirouette in the air with a downward pointing finger, and Julian Bernstein turned cooperatively and leaned against the wall and allowed himself to be patted down and handcuffed. Irene holstered her gun and read him his rights.

"My, my, my," said Officer Egan.

⁂

Hours later, twilight in Cambridge, long after having called Jet Blue to cancel her return, and calling Wanda to explain the delay on the east coast to question a suspect, her cell phone rang. It confounded her that the phone could work here on the east coast, receive a call from Mason County three thousand miles away, when she couldn't pick up a signal or receive an incoming call in Mason County itself. It didn't compute. She thought about the signal relayed from tower to tower like a ping-pong ball, crossing the Rockies, bouncing over the plains, across the Mississippi, rolling up the Ohio River valley and popping over the Alleghenies and Appalachians to vibrate the phone on her belt here where she sat in a hot, dreary interrogation room in Cambridge, Mass.

It was Giles Yates, one of her department's detectives who was working on the narcotics investigation with the Kitsap County officers, calling to report that he'd manufactured an excuse to drop in on Patrick McGrath, who was jumpy as hell and probably hiding *something*, whether it was a grow operation or a human bite along his jaw. He had a four-day stubble and if there was a laceration his beard was concealing it, and should he trump something up and bring him in for closer inspection?

"Don't worry about it," she told him, "let's drop it. Thanks for trying." She didn't care. She'd had blood drawn before she left. It was only for information since there was nothing wrong in her mouth suggesting she was vulnerable and nothing to be done in any case; but still, she'd tasted his blood and it scared her and she wanted to know. They'd draw blood again in thirty days and again after ninety, and then she'd be in the clear. Or not. She wanted the whole thing behind her.

She'd walked out into the hall to take the call, tired and glad of the break, the excuse to leave the room. She walked the length of the hall and dialed Victor. He answered and reported that he'd just gotten off work and he was by himself and when was she coming home? As soon as she could get on a flight, she told him—and what would he have for supper? Sausages he'd brought home from the store. Please walk the dog. Anything else new?

"That guy came by again," he said, "Theo."

"What's up with that?" she asked.

"I think he's more interested in you than in me, Mom," he said.

A bird fluttered in her chest, then closed its wings. She ignored it. Victor saw her differently now, she realized, no longer as just his mother, part of the furniture of his world, but suddenly as a separate person, a woman, with a constellation of her own, others in orbit besides him, and potential perils and promises. An exponential leap in growing up.

"I don't think he's going to prosecute us," he added.

"Is that what he said?"

"Well, not exactly."

"Well, what exactly did he say?" she asked.

"He didn't say anything really. I think he wanted to know where you were."

"And what did you say?" she asked.

"I said you were working."

"Okay," she said, "I am."

"'Bye," he said.

"I love you," she replied.

"Okay," he said. And hung up.

She walked back down the hall. Julian Bernstein had been right, the cuffs weren't necessary. He wasn't dangerous, wasn't a flight risk. He was amenable and cooperative. She had sat for hours in the small, windowless interrogation room at the Cambridge Police Department headquarters asking questions, listening to his answers, and now, after it all, she had nothing—no compelling evidence that he caused any harm to Anne Paris that would justify an arrest. Just his proximity, which alone was not enough, and his strangely obsessional relationship with Anne. She couldn't hold him. She was going to have to let him go. What she did know was his story, which had come out slowly at first, in terse answers to her questions, then in a raw, confessional rush that sounded truthful and unedited.

XXIII

Initially, Julian Bernstein didn't think he liked Anne. She'd come to look at the apartment. A tall girl, and taller still in platform sandals, with streaked blonde hair, disorganized as though she'd just gotten out of bed, long bangs falling into her eyes, wisps along her collarbone, surprisingly dark brows like crow's wings above arresting blue eyes level with his own. And young, a decade and a half his junior, just beginning a psychiatric residency. Not pretty exactly, he said, but very assured and self-possessed. Her voice was husky and melodic, and soft so that when she spoke you had to lean in to hear, and he felt drawn against his will, tilting his head to hers. He was annoyed when she laid her hand on his arm. Then she was all business. She ran the water in the shower and said the pressure was low and the drain was slow. It would have to be fixed. She looked in the oven and under the sink and said her boyfriend would have to leave his bicycle in the downstairs hall unless there was covered parking where it could be locked up. They would paint, she said, but he would have to supply the materials, and no, she would not agree to his approval of the color, it would be shades of white in any case. A princess, he thought, and who does she think she is? But she wrote a check for the first and last months' rent and he gave her the key, wondering what he was in for. In imagination he lay in bed listening to the clack of her heels crisscrossing the ceiling overhead, tracking her movements while sleep eluded him.

He felt, he said, afraid she would take advantage of him somehow, afraid that he shouldn't have allowed her in and that she'd gained a purchase in his world that put him in some way in jeopardy, and so he watched her. He listened for her car, for her footsteps on the stairs and the rush of water in the pipes in the walls signaling a bath or a shower or the toilet flushing. At night he noticed the lights from the rooms of her apartment going on and off reflected on the limbs of the trees growing next to the house. Her mail came through the slot in the front door along with his own, and he read the names of the senders as he sorted hers into a bowl on the hall tree. He learned to recognize the handwriting of her parents and he knew the catalogue companies she ordered from and the magazines she subscribed to.

She paid the rent on time and she and Ira made small improvements to the apartment, adding wooden blinds and bookcases that Ira installed and painted so they looked built-in and original. Their days were long and they came and went separately, Ira on the bicycle and Anne in her Subaru.

Sometimes Julian smelled cooking and could tell what they were having for dinner, curry or a roasted chicken. Rarely, friends came over and there was music and laughter overhead and Julian could neither concentrate nor sleep. Once, when he went up to protest, Anne gave him a seductive, reproachful look and took his arm, drawing him in, putting a glass in his hand, introducing him to the guests as 'the disturbed landlord from downstairs.' Disturbed. Disturbed how, he wondered? It wasn't clear. Disturbed by the noise or disturbed as a term of art, his mental state? Did she know he listened and watched? He wondered if he had been found out. Or had she ascertained something about him he didn't know himself and made a diagnosis?

He was, he knew, very much alone. He had been divorced for a long time and his last girlfriend had left several years before. In Anne's apartment—his apartment, really, if you thought about it, the top of his house—he felt awkward and out of place and wondered how to leave. Just walk out the door, he said to himself. Say 'goodnight' and 'keep it down' and leave. But he didn't. He lingered and drank too much red wine, talking to no one in any meaningful sense in any way that he could remember, watching. Later, Latin music pulsing, Anne climbed onto the coffee table and danced an exuberant, uninhibited salsa, her high heels castanets on the trunk lid, sinuous arms outstretched. Julian was mesmerized by the twitch of her hips. When the party broke up he left feeling agitated and confused. He didn't know if he'd been welcomed or been had. He wished he hadn't gone up. Perhaps, he thought, he should ask them to leave.

But he didn't, and they stayed, completing their residencies and beginning their respective practices. One spring evening she came home, pulled up in front of the house but didn't get out of the car. Julian was on his way out. He walked past her Subaru on the way to his Saab and glanced in her driver's side window and saw she was crying, her face flushed and contorted, cheeks sheeted with tears, eyes red as she looked up at him, her assurance dissolved, her fearsomeness evaporated. He bent to look in at her. "What?" he said, opening the door, and she wagged her head mutely and stepped out and into his arms, sobbing against his shirt. When he got the story, which was later in the darkness of his bedroom after much fierce, then tender, lovemaking—a performance he would not have thought himself capable of—it was a sad litany of Ira's infidelities, irresponsibilities, and ambivalence.

So, he said, began their affair. She would break things off with Ira, she promised, but not until the summer, after her boards. For the moment she needed calm in which to study, the status quo, with the addition of the excitement of their secret and the anticipation of the life they would build together. Julian bought Anne an extravagant diamond, which she accepted but wouldn't wear. Not yet, but soon, she promised.

Julian admitted he was baffled and angry and could not fathom why they had to wait and why he was required to share her for the interminable interim until the end of summer when her boards were behind her.

And, in fact, not long after she departed with Ira for the west coast and the annual month of summer vacation with her family at her beloved island, the wait became unendurable, and he followed. It was unplanned, he said, impulsive. He looked at Gustavus Island on Google Earth and zoomed in until he could pick out the roof of the Paris house and see the slough and the dune and the sandbar, all as she had described. He Map-Quested the address, bought a ticket and flew west. He rented a car and called her when he got cell reception, which was on the dirt road by the mailboxes. She came flying up the drive and out of the tunnel of trees, barefoot and tanned and blonde and wildly thrilled to see him, locking her pelvis into his and sinking her tongue into his mouth, but he couldn't stay, his presence mustn't be discovered. Quick! She knew a place. She slid behind the wheel and spun the car in a doughnut of sprayed gravel and hightailed it out to the blacktop. She turned off the county road into an overgrown lane at a trailhead that his eye would have missed, and nosed the car through huckleberry and salal and bracken ferns beneath towering firs, branches leaning in, raking the paint. She knew all the paths and all the secret places—she had roamed the island since childhood—and she parked in the woods and took Julian's hand and led him through the underbrush and into the clearing of the Donley cabin. They used the tire iron to pry open the door and climbed into the loft together and inaugurated their hideaway. Here, she said, he could stay undetected. He could shop in Shelton, buy groceries and books and anything else he needed, he could read and write and she would visit every day and every night. She would slip away and walk or sail to him.

And it was, as she promised, a secret summer idyll.

～✿～

THE EVENING of the squall Julian was on the beach watching for her when the I-14 rounded the point, flying before the wind, wing on wing on a green sea. The wind was ferocious, roaring south, pushing towering dark clouds, soughing in the firs growing on the lip of the bluff above. Julian could hear the trunks creak and groan and he wondered if it was safe where he stood. This was the kind of wind that toppled trees.

As he watched, Anne tried to tack toward shore and the boom swung, the sails flapped, then filled, and the boat heeled violently and he could tell she had lost control. He watched the I-14 swamp and go over, and when the mast hit the water he kicked off his shoes and plunged into the waves. He made a shallow dive and came up in a strong crawl toward the capsized vessel. He caught sight of her head intermittently between the waves as he swam toward her. When he reached her she was coughing and laughing, clinging to the boat.

"The tiller snapped," she yelled. It wasn't her fault but Leland was going to kill her and they should try to swim the boat to shore, otherwise who knew where it would end up. She had to shout to be heard. They grabbed the gunwales and pulled, kicking hard and swimming with one arm, trying to tow the boat, but the wind was sweeping them south, beyond the mouth of the Donley canyon toward the next point, the tip of the island beyond, and the open water of Dana Passage. Julian was cold and hampered by his clothing. Lightning flashed in the incoming front, and thunder rumbled.

"Let go," he shouted, prying at her fingers, "we have to get out of the water," pulling at her, grabbing her arms hard above the elbows, yanking, breaking her grasp, turning her toward the beach.

She didn't want to leave the boat—"No!" she shouted, "you never leave the boat," fighting against him. But the storm was nearly on top of them and he jerked her hands loose and the I-14 was swept out of her grasp.

Even swimming hard, when they finally reached shore they'd been carried well south and they had to wade, waist-deep in the waves, clambering over the spars, chilled and silent. It had started to rain, wind-driven sheets, and the canyon, when they reached it, had become a slippery torrent. They made their way upward, grabbing branches and saplings for handholds. Overhead a freight train roared through the firs.

Finally back at the cabin, they stripped off their wet clothes, hung them from the rafters, and Julian lit a fire. They huddled together in front of the stove wrapped in blankets, warming slowly, and sharing a bottle of good red wine Anne had brought that they'd been saving.

She was quiet and remote, unhappy about the end of their adventure and the fate of her brother's I-14, and in her silence Julian read reproval, as though she mistook his good judgment for faintheartedness, which wounded his pride, and so a chasm yawned between them.

Later, when the rain had stopped and the wind had died and their clothes were dry, they dressed and walked through the woods together. He wouldn't let her go back alone. He gave her his fleece jacket to put over her shoulders. They walked in silence, Indian file along the path, Julian following the pale scissoring of her bare legs, then hand in hand when the track opened up and they could walk abreast.

No lights were on at the Paris house or in the barn or study when they came down the drive, but even so they crept behind the barn and circled past the old outhouse. It was late by then and the tide would have receded and Julian wanted to walk back by the beach—it would be quicker that way. Anne walked with him down through the orchard and out to the dune and they kissed in the moonlight, a long, thoughtful, healing kiss. She pulled back and smiled and he could see the glint of her teeth, the whites of her eyes. They could make love, she said, right here, right now, on the dune. His heart soared in gratitude—whatever chill had come between them was gone. She slipped out of his jacket and spread it on the sand and pulled him down with her. It was quick and sweet and wordless, just her breath and gasp and his own hoarse moan.

A little later, looking back as he walked away, he could see the pale forms of her arms and legs—she wouldn't keep his jacket, no way of explaining it she said—luminous in the darkness where she stood watching him go. One arm lifted and waved. He waved back and walked on. When he looked again he could no longer see her, but he saw the flare of a match. Smoking, he thought, a cigarette before going up to bed. He walked on, tired, satisfied and already looking forward to tomorrow.

But the next day she didn't come.

"And the rest you know, Detective Chavez," he said. "I tried calling, couldn't reach her. I called the house. I was frantic, of course, and quite helpless. And angry, if you want to know. Yes, there had been a little rift, but we'd mended things. I was furious that she would just vanish without a word of explanation." A pause. "Then I talked to you," his voice cracking.

He shrugged slightly, looking at her. She relived that early morning call, remembering what he'd said and what she had said. Thinking back she was sure that Julian had been completely and genuinely stunned when she told him Anne was dead. He'd had other things to hide—his whereabouts and his relationship to Anne—but that she was dead, he hadn't known. His whole account sounded entirely plausible.

"Do you smoke?" she asked.

He looked at her, surprised. "I used to," he replied, "not anymore."

"But Anne smoked," she said.

"A little."

"Where did she get the cigarette?"

"What?" he asked.

"You said she was smoking as you walked away. Where did she get the cigarette?"

"What do you mean?"

"Where'd the cigarette come from? She'd been soaked to the skin, her cigarettes were in the boat."

He shot her a wary glance. "I didn't make that up."

"No, I believe you," she said. "But how do you know it was her?"

He swung his head around sharply. "Whoever struck that match was standing where I left her."

"Right," said Irene.

He studied her in silence, then shuddered slightly. "That's creepy," he said.

Irene was thinking of Ira, who had admitted to a night-time cigarette on the beach. Or Elliot or Libby or Rueben Guevara. Any one of them, or anyone, hidden in darkness on the edge of the slough, watching. "Where exactly was she when you left her?" Irene asked.

"We came out on the path," he said, "and that's where she kissed me, but then we walked a little, just a bit north and up into the dune grass." He was quiet for a long time, thinking. "There could have been cigarettes in my jacket pocket," he said finally. "I bought a pack to keep at the cabin. She didn't smoke much but she liked one now and then. She could have taken that pack when we left and put it in her pocket. Or in her shorts pocket. I don't remember. If she did, it didn't register with me."

"She gave the jacket back to you, Dr. Bernstein, and there were no pockets in her shorts," said Irene.

He was quiet.

❦

He was free to go. He declined the offer of a ride home in a cruiser, and she shook his hand, thanked him for his cooperation, apologized for the inconvenience, and promised to call if there was news. But he lingered for a moment, as though undecided, then offered to buy her a drink—it was painful, he said, and there was no one but her who knew about him and Anne and no one to talk to. "There's a place just around the corner."

"Not a good idea," said Irene, but still she was sorry for him and she almost changed her mind when he turned and pushed out through the double doors, letting in a wall of heat.

Sean Egan was at her shoulder. "Hey, boss, knock one back with the boys before you go?" he asked. "I'm off shift."

Irene smiled. "He asked me the same thing." Sean Egan had come and gone through the afternoon while she questioned Julian Bernstein.

"I know, I heard," he said. "There's a place just around the corner."

"No," she said, smiling. "But thanks."

⌘

IRENE SAT in the break room and called the airline and waited interminably on hold before she finally got an agent and found a flight home with an open seat. With an hour yet to kill, she signed out at the desk, stepped into the hot evening, and walked down the block and around the corner. Green neon advertising Rolling Rock spilled into the twilight. She stepped inside with her head down. She didn't want to see Julian Bernstein sitting alone at a table or at the end of the bar, or catch Sean Egan's eye in the back bar mirror, but she did want a drink before heading to the airport. She asked for an Irish whiskey and carried it over to the jukebox. She felt unmoored and a long way from home, present in other people's lives like a space traveler in an alien world where everyone else knew the conventions. She punched in a Bruce Springsteen ballad to ground her in a more familiar universe. *My name is Joe Roberts/I work for the state . . .* and the harmonica's wail.

There was a touch on her shoulder. Sean Egan, standing at her side. "It's the Boss," he said, smiling, and she wasn't sure if he meant her or Bruce Springsteen. All in one motion he lifted the glass of whiskey out of her fingers, set it on the jukebox, took her hand in his, laced an arm around her waist, swung her in close, guiding her backwards into a two-step, then looped her out in a turn under his arm and reeled her back in again. It felt good to be dancing, moving to the music with someone's hands on her. She liked Sean Egan, she realized, liked his calm irony and liked that he knew exactly what he wanted. She wondered how you got to be like that when you were still so young. She found herself checking for a ring. There was none. She wondered if he was even out of his twenties, and didn't think so. It was a good thing, she thought, that she'd booked that flight, because otherwise, if he'd asked, and she thought he might, she would be tempted to tarry in Beantown.

They didn't dance the night away, but they danced until she had to go. Her shirt was soaked beneath her jacket, the holster under her arm pasted to her side, her face flushed and her hair hanging in damp tendrils. He walked her out to find her car and kissed her softly before she got in. "You're a good one, boss," he said.

XXIV

Irene heard the mower somewhere down in the orchard. She glanced in the barn as she walked past. No Triumph. She should not have let Ira go. She was kicking herself. She wondered where he would have gotten to by now. Time was turning somersaults. Somewhere above the Great Lakes rolling through the wheat fields of Ontario. That is, if he was going where he said he was going, which was a completely unreliable assumption. Now she could picture the apartment he was going home to—if he was going home. He could just as easily have crossed the border directly north into Vancouver and be building a new identity. Or be on a plane somewhere bound for a new life. She'd let him go scot-free out of the country. That, among other things, was going to take some explaining if he didn't turn up in Boston in a couple of days. She wondered if he did, if Julian Bernstein would let him keep the apartment if he wanted to.

And she wondered if Ira knew about Julian and Anne, had known or suspected all along, if that knowledge and Anne's du-- plicity festered and poisoned him. She wondered if it was Ira's match Julian had seen as he walked away. Ira lighting a ciga- rette after whacking Anne on the back of the head with a rock or a length of iron-hard driftwood. Maybe Ira had stood in the dark on the edge of the slough watching his girl kissing the land- lord, watched them lie down on the dune and make love, heard her gasp and seen her smile. She wondered if he'd walked up behind her as she straightened her clothes, overcome by rage and jealousy, whacked her on the head, then slipped her limp body into the slough as Julian walked away. Because, if Julian was telling the truth, and Irene believed he was, Anne was alive and well on the dune long after the storm and the wreck of the I-14, which confirmed, for Irene at least, that Anne's death could not have been accidental and had happened there, where her body was found.

She had to reorder everything she knew now, reassemble her hypotheses to include the new information, everything she'd learned in Boston. It was brain-numbing. She had fit pieces of a puzzle together so things made sense, and all of a sudden there was a new element to incorporate and she had to begin again, deconstruct the theories she'd developed back into a random collection of bits of information. She wondered what else she might have missed and what other assumptions she'd made without even knowing.

She shouldn't have let Ira go. He had migrated to the top of her list and was now her prime suspect.

She walked into the dimness of the barn and looked around. The cot was there, the oyster shell ashtray, the prescription vial— the books and sleeping bag gone. Irene sat down on the cot and read the label on the little amber bottle. Flagyl. The medicine for giardia. He'd had it too then. She tried to remember if she'd drunk the water. She had. She remembered now the jar of water Libby gave her, still water with a slice of lemon—was that out of the tap or something that came out of a bottle? At the lunch on the bluff, now seemingly so long ago but really less than a week, there had been Pellegrino in green bottles. She couldn't remember what she'd had then. She knew she hadn't drunk the wine, though she'd wanted to. She wondered how long it took for giardia to make itself known. She felt slightly queasy thinking about it.

❧

IRENE WALKED on down into the orchard toward the racket of the mower. It was Libby, as Irene had supposed, at the bottom of the orchard attacking a last unmown corner of pasture behind the slough where the grass was waist-high. Libby leaned down on the handle, rearing the mower up on the oversized back wheels, then advanced, lowering the blade onto the standing grass. It looked like punishing work, and the noise it made was a relentless roar. Irene wondered why she did it, why the family didn't just hire someone with a tractor. It wasn't as though they couldn't afford it. It seemed bizarre that Libby would undertake to do it. She was on *vacation*.

Libby was wearing jeans and a faded blue tee shirt, sodden with sweat, a pith helmet draped with mesh on her head. Her arms were lean and darkly tanned. She hadn't seen Irene approaching, and Irene stood in the shade of a pear tree some distance back, watching. She thought about what Elliot had said, that Libby was born with teeth, and how unsettling that would be.

Suddenly Libby yelled and let go of the mower—the dead man switch killed the engine when she released the throttle bar and silence settled. She was stumbling backwards, slapping at her arms, then turning and running.

A sting on the side of her own neck, and Irene understood— wasps, nesting in the ground, and Libby had mown over the hive—now she was running too, side by side with Libby, running pell-mell uphill between the rows of trees. Didn't they say not to run, Irene thought—stop and roll into a ball—or was that in a bear attack? It didn't matter, instinct ruled and they were running as if their lives depended on it, angry wasps swarming after them. Libby tore off her helmet as she ran—wasps caught in the mesh—and flung it.

Up behind the barn, beyond the orchard and into the open pasture, they slowed and stopped, breathless, bending over, hands braced on knees, panting, checking behind themselves. But the wasps had stopped too—some sort of territorial limit had been reached. Irene straightened and then, looking at Libby, grabbed her hand and swept away wasps stuck all along her arm, wrist to shoulder, welts already rising.

She shook her head—something buzzing in her own hair.

Libby yanked off her shirt—wasps stuck and stinging through the cloth, and snapped it like a wet towel. They turned wordlessly for each other's inspection, Libby thin as a boy in a black bra, her back a washboard of stung ribs.

Libby's face was flushed and sheeted with tears, her eyes red. She'd been crying, Irene realized, even before the wasp attack. She didn't even pretend to compose herself—she pulled her shirt back on and sat down and put her head in her arms.

"Can I do something?" asked Irene.

Libby wagged her head.

"Baking soda? Benadryl?"

"It isn't that. It's not that bad," said Libby, her voice choked and muffled. "I'm not allergic or anything." But she was pale and shivering, some sort of reaction setting in.

"Elliot?"

At that, Libby lifted her head, looking at Irene. "Ha!" she spat, her eyes narrow, her face furious, "No, not Elliot."

What's up with that, wondered Irene. She was silent for a while, sitting in the pale stubble of mown grass, contemplating the snow-covered majesty of the Olympic range rising in the distance beyond the orchard, Libby weeping beside her. She wanted to use the moment, auger in while Libby was undefended, ferret out the reason for her rage—because these were angry, helpless tears, this wasn't grief, it was fury. Something had happened and Irene wanted to know what. "What's up?" she asked finally, lamely.

Libby looked up and sluiced her cheeks with the sides of her palms. "I hate this," she said. "I hate it," her arm making a sweeping, inclusive gesture encompassing the orchard, the barn, the house, the bluff. "What a sham, what a lie. Everything's a sham. My whole family, my life."

She was quiet then, her outburst over, her tears drying. But after a moment she glanced at Irene, calmer now, picking at a welt on her arm.

"You want to know something?"

"Sure," said Irene.

"The giardia everyone's had?"

"Yes?" said Irene.

"It isn't giardia."

Irene thought about the mouse that Nikki said had fallen into the well and drowned there, contaminating the water, making anyone who drank it sick with the same nasty protozoa you might catch camping in the mountains if you drank stream water— beaver fever they used to call it. Or something you got in Mexico, a more severe version of *turista*, lingering sometimes long after you came home, tiny creatures swimming in your gut, making you intermittently sick. She thought of the little amber bottles of Flagyl in everyone's medicine chest.

"No?" said Irene.

"No," said Libby.

"What then?"

⸺⧉⸺

Sʜᴇ'ᴅ ʜᴀᴅ, Libby said, some odd and unpleasant symptoms and she'd talked to Nikki, a gynecologist after all—that's what they'd been talking about that day on the beach, the consultation, remember?—and Nikki wrote a prescription which Libby filled in town, for herself and for Elliot. He should take it too, her husband. She didn't question why. She hadn't, Libby said, thought much about it one way or the other. Mostly she'd focused on the recommendation not to drink alcohol while taking the medication, because she liked to have a beer in the afternoon and wine with dinner and it would be hard to give that up, though only for two days, a short course of treatment. But then—and this was the revelation—it registered—probably something she had known all along on some level but hadn't consciously acknowledged—that the prescription was the same as the prescription Elliot had been given earlier, also by Nikki, for, he said, giardia.

A busman's holiday Dr. Roth was having out here in the Pacific Northwest where the Walmart pharmacy didn't have to honor her credentials, but did, filling prescriptions for Flagyl for Anne and Ira—Julian Bernstein too, when Irene investigated further—and

Elliot and Libby. At the time, Libby remembered, Elliot had said she should take it too, prophylactically, which she thought was silly, and which she didn't do. She wasn't sick and she wasn't drinking the water and she didn't understand why he was worried. If she'd done as he suggested—taken the medicine then, she said now—she would never have known.

A protozoa, it turned out, caused giardia, if you drank contaminated water, but a similar protozoa in the reproductive tract caused an equally nasty condition, trichomoniasis, which had nothing to do with drinking water. Trich, as Nikki abbreviated it, was something you caught from an infected sexual partner. The mouse in the well, Libby said, was a ruse, a fabrication—so plausible, such a marvelous subterfuge—who dreamed that up? Anne and Nikki, putting their heads together and concocting a fable—'You won't believe what happened this summer, we couldn't drink the well water.' And no one drank the well water. They drank Pellegrino and wine, and lemonade out of cartons for the kids, and no one suspected, no one questioned, no one asked for water quality testing. They just laughed and joked about the exigencies of summer houses and country living and feigned concern that Oliver might forget and drink the water. Giardia would be hard on an older person. So brash and clever. Something so simple and obvious that later Irene couldn't imagine she'd overlooked it. The truth hiding in plain sight, right there in the open for anyone to see. The kind of mistake she was trained not to make.

XXV

The fight, Libby said, had started over something else. Namely, money. No surprise, most couples fought over money. Elliot had come back from L.A. flush with success, sure he'd get the part, and he'd rented the car in Portland, which they couldn't afford—he should have let the airline bus him up to Sea-Tac and driven his own car home—and then—and this was what she'd been ragging on him about—he hadn't gotten it back. The Neon was still sitting out there in the grass beside the barn, every day another day of the bill mounting, while their own old Volvo station wagon, which he'd left in the airport garage—an outlying lot and a shuttle van being all too plebeian—was racking up its own tab. She didn't understand.

They were all sad and preoccupied, but there wasn't anything anyone could do. Elliot didn't need to *be* here. He could have returned the car. He could have gotten out of bed and into the Neon, driven to Sea-Tac and been back in a matter of hours. He could have taken the boys and made a day of it, taken them hiking on Mount Rainier. They might have opened up in the car, talked about how they were feeling. He could have used some initiative, thought of someone besides himself. He might have considered her and the boys, the impact of everything on them. But he didn't think that way. He thought only of himself and his own hand-wringing angst over professional rejection and his desire for a cigarette and his need for a drink. He sat by the phone like a girl—not literally sitting by the phone but you know what I mean, Libby said—waiting for his agent to call, not taking care of business. And she was tired of it. She was stretched thin to breaking.

It made her low and downhearted when Elliot was disappointed, knowing but still hoping, refusing to call the agent himself, but she had her own disappointment—God, they needed the money that job would bring, and the psychological boost—and she couldn't keep him up all the time. It was like keeping a balloon in the air and trying to do everything else at the same time, the dishes and housework, helping the kids with their homework, reconcile the checkbook and decide which bills to pay, all the while one eye on the balloon, making sure to keep it up, giving it her full attention whenever it threatened to sag. She couldn't do it anymore. Someone needed to make a living, and substitute teaching wasn't enough. And she, Libby said, wanted a drink too but couldn't because of the medication she was taking. At that point in their arguing, she said, the light bulb went on.

Libby went silent. She compared the prescriptions—his little vial, empty now but still there on the floor by the mattress, and hers, the tablets he'd given her which she hadn't taken, and the new prescription from Nikki, which she'd filled in town, and its twin for him. Identical dose, same instructions. Her heart was fluttering and she couldn't catch her breath. They had to fight in undertones because the boys were sleeping at the other end of the loft.

"It wasn't giardia, was it?" she asked.

"What?" he said.

"You didn't take *this* for *giardia*," looking at him, shaking the bottle in front of his face. "*You* had what I've got."

"I don't know what you mean," he said, looking baffled. It made her furious.

"Who?" she demanded.

"Who what?" answered Elliot.

She wanted to strangle him. She wanted to hit him, flail out, smack him. "Let's see," she said instead, her voice a steely parody of deduction, heavy on the irony, "who's had 'giardia'?" She ticked them off her fingers. "Ira. Anne. You. And now, me."

Elliot was kneeling in the middle of the bed behind her. She felt his hands come down gently on her shoulders and she shrugged him off, turning fiercely toward him. "Don't lie to me," she spat.

He sat back looking dumb and wounded, tears glistening in his eyes in the light of the candle lantern. "Libby," he said, "I would *never* have done that to you."

"What? Done what?"

"What you think. What you're saying."

"I'm not saying anything. I'm asking *who*?"

The tears spilled over, looking at her, shaking his head slowly, emphatically. "No," he said. "Never."

"Anne," Libby said. "My *sister*. How could you?"

⊸⟨⟩⊸

I<small>T HAD</small> gone on, Libby said, Elliot protesting, she pressing, pushing for a confession, hoping for an explanation or some sort of plausible fabrication she could believe in, both of them crying, until she heard the boys stir and turn, even in their sleep hearing the ragged edge in their parents' hushed voices. She pulled the comforter off the mattress and stalked out of the loft and down the stairs, into the barn where she lay down on Ira's cot. She lay awake wondering what was to become of her, her marriage, her children, of life as she knew it. When the sky was lightening, she heard Elliot on the stairs. He went out through the granary and she watched his silhouette as he walked past the open barn door without seeing her. But in a few minutes he was back, searching for her. He came in and sat on the foot of the cot and reached for her hand.

"It was only once," he said. "Anne was crying. We were here in the barn. She was sitting on the steps to the granary over there. Something about Ira, and Julia being dead, and how lonely she was. I didn't mean to. I didn't start it. I just felt bad for her and I put my arm around her. And then we just . . ." He trailed off.

⌐⌐⌐

Lɪʙʙʏ ʟᴏᴏᴋᴇᴅ at Irene. "If Anne were alive, I'd want to kill her," she said. "She had everything, she didn't need my husband. I don't think she even wanted him, she just wanted to know she could have him. I'm sure it cheered her up. A little diversion for her. She was like that. All the toys in the sandbox." Her voice ragged.

If what Libby was saying were true, Irene thought, she had a powerful motive—rage and jealousy, sexual infidelity. Already she'd had much to resent—the discrepancy of paternal affection, the discrepancy of means and education, the presumed discrepancy of future inheritance—and now this, if this was true. But the timing didn't fit to make it a motive. If she was telling the truth, and Irene thought she was, Libby didn't know until now, just last night, days after Anne's death.

"Did you?" Irene asked.

"Did I what?"

"Did you kill her? Did you sneak up behind her and whack her on the back of the head with something heavy and shove her body into the slough?"

"No, I didn't."

They sat side by side in the mown field looking out at the distant mountains. Finally Libby said, "And I wouldn't have anyway. Because I loved her. That's why it's so confusing. How can you hate someone and love them at the same time? It's the way I feel about Elliot also."

"What will you do?" asked Irene after a while.

"I don't know," said Libby. "Maybe leave. Maybe nothing."

"Where's Elliot now?"

"He's returning the Neon, then taking the boys hiking."

They looked at each other. Libby didn't exactly smile but her expression softened into a kind of woeful irony. She was pale and shivering despite the heat, her face dirty and tracked by her tears. Irene could feel her own wasp sting on the side of her neck and one on her wrist, the venom in her system, chilling her too, making her a little light-headed and slightly nauseated. "What will you do about all these stings?"

"Swim, I guess." said Libby. "I wish there was a bathtub I could fill up with baking soda, but the salt water will help."

"Come on," said Irene, standing and reaching a hand to pull Libby to her feet. They headed toward the barn and for a moment, before she let go, Libby walked with Irene's hand in hers. In another world, Irene thought, they could be friends.

XXVI

Irene had left Libby at the barn and had gone in search of Nikki. She'd found her in the little guest room that was tucked under the eaves behind the kitchen, packing. "It's my last day," Nikki said. "Leland's driving me out to the highway to catch the county airporter."

"We need to talk," said Irene.

"Come," said Nikki, "I'm walking down to the Strausses' to say good-bye before I go." She zipped her suitcase closed and rolled it through the kitchen and out to the porch where she left it standing behind them as they walked down the orchard path.

Her investigation was coming to a close, Irene thought, everyone dispersing. Soon, within days, tomorrow even, she'd have to release the body, let Oliver Paris have his daughter's remains to cremate, transport, or bury here, if he could get permission.

"So," said Irene, "giardia?"

"Right," said Nikki.

"You've got some explaining to do."

"Right," said Nikki again.

They had taken off their shoes at the bottom of the orchard path—Nikki, in sleek black yoga pants, her traveling attire, slipping out of incongruous, impractical gladiator sandals, and Irene unlacing her boots and rolling up her black jeans. Now they walked far out on the sandy spit, the bluff and the house a long way back over their shoulders.

"The whole giardia thing was just a story we concocted when Anne realized she had something and there was more than one partner and people had to be treated and would ask questions," Nikki said.

"People like who?" asked Irene.

"Well, like Libby, for instance." Nikki looked carefully at Irene. "I don't think I'm telling you something you don't already know."

"No," said Irene.

"In the world of medicine you're not supposed to prescribe for yourself," said Nikki. "Most of the time no one cares, pharmacies will fill it—it's really just narcotics and opiates that make them jumpy—and you're really only supposed to prescribe in states where you're licensed. But most of the pharmacies don't care. If you've got a printed prescription pad with your license number on it, they'll fill it. But Oliver's old school about that kind of thing and Anne was too. Worried about questions, you know, raised eyebrows. Heaven forbid a rebuke. So when Anne had symptoms, she asked me for a prescription. She knew what it was—she's a doctor after all—and I knew what it was, and she thought she knew where it came from."

"Ecuador," said Irene.

"Right," said Nikki. "That's what Anne thought but she wasn't one hundred percent certain. With trich, women experience the symptoms, men don't even know they have it. So she was a little bit out on a limb when she accused Ira. But in Ecuador he'd had, what, an imbroglio? Is that what they call it?"

"Fandango is what he said to me," said Irene.

Nikki laughed. "Anne lucked out. He told her about the girl down there. He was abject, she was righteous. And then she had a reason for banishing him to the barn, which, to tell the truth, she'd been wanting to do anyway. So everyone was dosing themselves—well, not everyone, but Anne was, and Ira and then Elliot."

"And Julian Bernstein," Irene added.

Nikki shot her a glance. "Yes, Julian Bernstein, too. Which was a little weird."

"How so?" asked Irene.

"You're a good detective, aren't you?" Nikki asked.

"I am, yes," said Irene. "Thank you."

"I wasn't sure you had figured out about Julian Bernstein."

"And were you planning on telling me?" Irene asked.

Nikki flashed her a look. "Maybe. I don't know. It didn't seem pertinent and it seemed a little squalid."

"I like to decide for myself what's pertinent and what's not, and squalid is often pertinent," said Irene. "Anything else that's not pertinent that you're keeping to yourself?"

Nikki laughed. "I don't think so."

Irene eyed her, not at all certain that this was the case. "So what was the weird part about Julian Bernstein?"

"Oh, well, the only weird part was that she wanted to send him the pills. It just seemed odd to me, impractical. It would have been easier and faster to send the prescription. I could have faxed it from town. Or she could have. And in Boston there wouldn't have been any questions—I'm licensed in Massachusetts. She is too. But she wanted to fill it here and Fed-Ex him the tablets. It was just odd. Anne was maybe a bit of a control freak."

"You didn't know he was here, then?"

It was like dropping a bomb. Nikki stopped walking and looked at Irene. "Who?"

"Julian Bernstein."

"Here?" asked Nikki, incredulous.

"Here," said Irene.

"Where?" asked Nikki, disbelieving.

"Down the beach in an abandoned cabin."

"I don't believe you," said Nikki.

But Irene could tell she did.

"Anne told me everything. I was completely in her confidence," said Nikki.

"Apparently not," said Irene.

"*When* was he here?"

"Pretty much the whole time," said Irene. "He followed her out."

Nikki looked pained and disconcerted. "That would explain why she wanted to fill the prescription here then."

"You didn't suspect?"

"It never occurred to me," Nikki said. "Now of course it makes sense. Sometimes she'd go for a walk and wouldn't want me to come. She'd say she wanted to be alone. Sometimes she just wasn't around and I didn't know *where* she'd gone. I thought it was because she had a lot on her mind." Nikki was silent, looking into the distance, shaking her head. "Shrinks are trained to keep secrets," she said finally, "it's their job and they're used to it. Most people get uncomfortable keeping something from you and they just blurt it out. Not shrinks. They can keep the most outlandish things to themselves. But it was different with Anne and me. We'd been friends since freshman year in college. We told each other everything."

Nikki started walking again. "Anne had this way about her, which is very attractive to people, where she's sort of conspiratorial, like she's letting you in on something no one else knows? She comes in very close and gazes at you from under her eyes and lowers her voice and touches your arm. She's very seductive. She makes you feel special. I've watched her. But I didn't think she was doing that with *me*. I thought I was her best friend, her confidante. Me alone." She looked at Irene, baffled and stricken. "Everyone must have felt that way."

Irene had a glimpse then of what it was like to be duped by Anne Paris—dumbfounding, stupefying, enraging.

⋘◈⋙

THE STRAUSS cabin was exactly as Irene remembered from over twenty years before, a weathered box set on pilings above the sand surrounded by a deck with a catwalk leading to a vertiginous stairway ascending the bluff behind. At high tide the water came up under the house. She had an unnerving sense of déjà vu following Nikki up the stairs to the deck where Nigel and Peter were arranged in attitudes of torpor in decrepit wicker armchairs, an assortment of empty beer bottles, and a lump of cheese softening in the heat, attesting to their afternoon's activity.

"Come up, sit down," they welcomed, waving Nikki and Irene onto the porch where they dropped onto the bench that was built into the porch railing. "We're having a child-free day," said Peter. "Elliot's taken the boys hiking, the women have gone to town, and we've been utterly indolent." Without rising he reached sideways into a cooler and pulled out a couple of icy beers. Irene shook her head, but Nikki took one and twisted off the top.

"You remember Detective Chavez?" Nikki said.

The Strauss brothers nodded.

"How's it going down there?" asked Nigel. An open-ended question asked in a sympathetic tone.

Irene shrugged.

"It's ghastly," Nikki said.

"How's Oliver?"

"It's hard to know. You don't see him—he's holed up in his office except for meals, and then he eats without speaking. He's devastated. We're all sort of catatonic."

"What have you learned?" Nigel asked Irene.

"A lot of people could have done it. A lot of people might have wanted to."

"Not an accident then?"

"I don't think so," she said.

Nigel, Irene noticed, was looking at her oddly. "Moran," he said finally. "Irene Moran."

Irene nodded.

"I thought I knew you," he said. "It's been bothering me."

"Irene Moran?" asked Peter.

"Yes," she said.

Peter thought it over. "Shelton High. You were a year ahead of me."

"Right," said Irene, "Nigel's class."

"There was a reunion in June," said Nigel, "twenty years. You didn't go."

"No."

Nigel was studying her. "I went. It was pretty much as you'd expect. The ones who showed up were mostly pretty depressing.

Most of them are still here. They never left. Some of them are grandparents."

Irene smiled. "Whoa," she said.

"What's it like," he asked, "living here where you grew up?"

"It isn't what I expected," Irene answered, "but it's okay."

"What did you expect?"

"Something different." Nigel's assumptions irked her. He'd gone to college in Madison and taught there now, molecular biology or something, but still came back in the summers to the cabin on the island, the academic calendar affording him long summer holidays. She stood up. She needed to get off the porch, out of the past and back into her own life. Nikki could walk back alone.

XXVII

Irene stood at the end of the long dock at the Shelton Marina where the Coast Guard had tied up Leland's International 14 sailboat. One of the other deputies had been out and had taken a mold of the boom, and gone over the cockpit for evidence Irene might have missed when she looked it over earlier out at the island with the Coast Guard officer, but had found nothing. No hair or skin or traces of blood. The boat had been scoured by sand and salt water. Chesterine Reade and Felix Guzmán had both studied photographs of the boom and compared the plaster mold to the head injury, and they agreed that it was possible but unlikely that Anne had been struck and killed by the boom. Something a little less regular, a stick or a pipe with some sort of fitting was more likely in their view, their caution rendering their opinion less conclusive, and less helpful, than Irene would have wished.

Leland wanted his boat back. Other than the broken tiller handle and scrapes and dings to the paint and gunwales, the boat didn't have much damage. Leland had ordered a new tiller and wanted to install it and sail the boat home before his vacation came to a close. Furthermore, as soon as the Mason County Sheriff's Department released the vessel, it would start racking up moorage fees—per foot, per day—a situation Leland wanted to avoid. There was no reason not to comply with his request, and Irene had told him she'd stop by the marina to remove the padlock and crime scene tape so the boat would be available whenever he wished.

It was an elegant-looking craft with a narrow hull and tall mast. Standing there contemplating it on a hot, still evening, Irene tried to picture how it would have looked as Rueben Guevara and Julian Bernstein had described it, flying under full sail, wing on wing across a stormy sea. To her the image seemed more frightening than exhilarating, though listening to Leland, who was an avid sailor and was, by his own account, moderately accomplished in a certain class of boat, she realized sailing could become an obsession for some people. Not racing necessarily, but knowing your boat, learning to read the water and the wind and how to trim your sails exactly right to optimize performance. Leland applied science to everything—science was what he knew and was the prism through which he focused all his experience. He talked about the physics and geometry of sailing. He knew the arcane effects of principles like drag, displacement and sheer, words Irene understood in a much more general way.

Leland applied science to his theory of Anne's death too, a contrarian theory to Irene's mind which initially seemed out of character. Interestingly, Leland was convinced that Anne's death was accidental, that she had been sailing in conditions beyond her abilities, that she made a relatively small mistake—though fatal in her circumstance—a miscalculation of how much wind the sails could hold and how much torque the tiller could take. The tiller handle failed, she lost control, the boat jibed, the boom swung with all the force of the gale, striking Anne, crushing her skull and knocking her overboard.

Leland was attached to his theory and had thought it out carefully. He tested the facts of where Anne's body was found and where the I-14 went aground against his knowledge of the winds and tides of Case Inlet, and winds and tides in general. He had shown Irene the navigational charts for the inlet, showing the depths and the underwater topography. He talked persuasively about eddies and currents, sandbars and underwater rifts, the location where he thought the incident had occurred and what time in the evening it had happened. In his telling it sounded plausible and convincing, his science irrefutable. You could put him on the stand as an expert and imagine him persuading a jury.

In any event, Irene couldn't dispute the science even though she thought he was wrong. She had the benefit of Julian Bernstein's account, which she conditionally believed and which Leland hadn't heard—but she thought that Leland was oddly invested in the accidental theory and wondered why. He was not an emotional man. He seemed quite buttoned-up. He told you what he thought, and all the reasons why, but not what he felt. Irene wondered if the very scientific professor had behaved very unscientifically and had chosen the thesis he preferred and had then gone about proving its probability, rather than assessing the evidence first and arriving at a conclusion later.

Leland spoke with a kind of breathy urgency that made him seem anxious, but he was low on Irene's list of potential suspects and she thought his manner probably suggested nothing more than a characteristic need to convince.

"How do you feel about Anne's death," Irene had asked.

"I'm very worried about Oliver," had been his reply.

Later, when she asked Rosalie about it, Rosalie made an exasperated puffing sound through her lips and said, "He doesn't know *what* he feels. He doesn't *have* feelings." Her eyes filled and Irene realized she'd hit a nerve. Rosalie was very pent up too, for all her garrulousness. "I don't know what's wrong with him," she went on, "I just know that there's some terrible hurt that he won't deal with, won't even admit exists, something that goes way back. He's always been that way." You couldn't press him, she said, or he'd just retreat into silence. His view of the world, he maintained, was simply different, he didn't choose to speculate about what couldn't be measured or proven, so he left psychology and emotions to other members of the family. She herself, Rosalie said, was just totally and hopelessly ADHD, OCD—an alphabet soup that to her defined a whole universe of behavior. She just tried to stay focused. She was constructing a wood-fired pizza oven, she said, using entirely found materials.

Irene felt suddenly sorry for Rosalie—smart and talented, but not happy. She wondered if the pizza oven would ever be finished. She'd noticed the pile of bricks and broken concrete, and the beginning of an edifice rising out of the rubble out near the clothesline behind the kitchen.

⊰⊱

IRENE WAS wrapping things up. Tomorrow she would stop in at the morgue and sign the paperwork to release the body to the Paris family, and would make a last appointment with Chesterine.

⊰⊱

IN THE course of the day Irene had learned something about what Nikki called the 'art and science' of psychoanalysis. And she'd learned a good deal about Oliver Paris, his recently deceased wife Julia, and their daughter Anne, all practitioners of this arcane and misunderstood mental health subspecialty.

The art and science part, it seemed, as best as Irene could grasp, was a marriage of neurobiology—which was the measurable, observable science of the brain (which Freud had studied)—with a deeply sympathetic and intuitive interpretive pas-de-deux carried on through frequent (four times a week) and protracted (years long) sessions between patient and therapist in which the patient relived and came to understand seminal relationships and events, and with this new understanding got unstuck from old, trauma-induced, destructive patterns of behavior. It was an expensive and time-consuming enterprise, usually undertaken by comfortably fixed, highly intelligent, well-educated people.

It was not something Irene could easily fit into her vision of the practical and necessary conduct of normal everyday life. To her it sounded excessive and self-indulgent—endless hours spent thinking about and talking about oneself. You didn't go to a psychoanalyst for, say, anger management or trouble getting along with your boss—though sometimes those kinds of problems were the obvious presenting issues, and you had regular psycho-therapy for a while until the psychoanalyst began to think that perhaps your problems went deeper and that you would benefit from the analytic experience.

Most people wrestled with issues as they came up without re-visiting childhood trauma and were, in the psychoanalyst's nomen-clature, "well-defended." That is, they had built up useful defenses that worked adequately to shield them from old wounds.

Irene, looking back on her own childhood, couldn't imagine what experiences had made her into the self she'd become. She felt more like a product of her own desires and determinations than of her parents' upbringing and the events of her early childhood, a deliberate growing up and away that culminated with separa-tion, going away, in those first giddy days after high school. She didn't remember a whole lot about her early years—the tragedy of a cat that vanished and never came back when she was four, the television always on in their house with no one watching until her father came home from work and parked himself in front of it in 'his' chair, a place no one sat but him.

Sometimes though, she remembered, he'd haul her up into his lap and she'd lie there in the cradle of his arm, sucking her thumb, watching the flickering screen. He smelled of pitch and tobacco and damp wool. In her memory it was dark outside and the lights were on in their house and the kitchen windows were steamed up. There had been neighborhood friends and hide-and-seek on summer evenings, and four square and hopscotch in the street after school. Not a bad childhood—her parents had left her mostly alone—but they had nothing much to do with who she was now.

XXVIII

Theo was on the foredeck when he heard a clatter on the gangway that connected the parking lot to the dock. He looked up and saw Irene Chavez descending onto the pier. He busied himself with the caulking he was doing to forestall a hatch leak. In his sudden pleasure and confusion it didn't occur to him that there could be a reason besides him that she'd be there at the Shelton Marina, but she walked on past his slip without a hail or even a glance, as far as he could tell. He watched her back retreating along the pier, feeling deflated and foolish. What was she doing here?

When she stopped at the end of the long dock at the last slip, he remembered someone saying that there was an impounded boat the Coast Guard had towed in for forensic testing. He hadn't put it together at the time, but now he did—the sailing accident—or homicide—out on Gustavus Island that she was investigating. Nothing to do with him. It took him down a peg, but made him smile at himself too—the ricochet of feelings between certainty and disappointment and the corresponding burgeoning of desire.

Theo had come home at the end of a long day, climbed out of his suit and into a pair of shorts and an ancient tee shirt and had immediately addressed himself—while there was still a window of daylight—to a long-neglected list of tasks he needed to accomplish to winterize his vessel before the rains. It was August and the mercury was well into the eighties, the moisture sucked out of everything, impossible to imagine the coming sodden months;

but every desiccated, shrunken bead of caulk around every hatch and fitting or window would be an invitation for dampness to penetrate and black mold to follow.

Now though, his ambition was derailed. Winterizing the trawler could wait. Irene Chavez may not have descended onto the pier to visit him, but it was a propitious moment and he was not going to let it pass him by.

⁓⊙⊱⁓

"Detective Chavez," he said behind her. Irene turned. For a moment she didn't recognize him—out of his suit and wearing shorts and, more startlingly, red Crocs on his feet, tanned and disheveled and here so unexpectedly, out of context and hard to place.

"What are *you* doing here?" she asked.

"I live here," he said.

"Live here?"

"I have a boat. I live aboard."

"Oh," she said. "Live aboard? Live on a boat?"

"I do," he said. "Before this I fished in Alaska for a while. Did you know that?"

"I'm not sure I did," she said. "I think I would have remembered."

Irene was sure she would have remembered, and certain that she hadn't heard anything about Theo Choate's background to suggest that he'd ever done anything other than law. She was enough her father's daughter to have an automatic respect for anyone who did hard and dangerous work—fishing definitely qualified—and that hadn't been part of her picture of the new Mason County prosecutor. She tilted her head a bit, adjusting her assumptions and looking at him with new eyes, a little more interested suddenly in knowing something about him other than what he was going to do about Victor.

"I tried to sell my boat up there but couldn't find a buyer," he went on. "Everyone's trying to get out, no one's buying in.

⁓ 185 ⊱⁓

There's not the money in fishing anymore. No one wants a boat."
He smiled ruefully. "So I brought it down here. It's just down the
dock." He jerked his head, "Slip twenty-three. An old trawler. I'll
show you."

There was a chain and a padlock as well as the mooring lines
attaching the I-14 to the dock, and Irene knelt without answering
and opened the lock and hauled the chain loose of the fittings,
then she straightened up and ripped away the yellow crime tape,
wadding it into a ball. Leland was now free to claim his boat.

"Okay," she said then, and followed Theo back down the
dock to slip twenty-three where she stopped and regarded Theo's
unprepossessing vessel. It looked like what it was, a work boat in
not terribly good repair. He offered her a hand and she stepped
aboard.

"Do you want a tour?" he asked.

"Sure," she said.

It didn't take long. Down the ladder into the galley, astern
to the crew bunk room he'd converted into a living space where
there were bookcases and a vintage chrome and leather lounge
chair positioned beside a small wood-burning stove. Then forward to the head and the vee berth where he slept.

To Irene it seemed quite foreign and exotic—cramped, but
appealing. He was tidy for the most part, though the bed wasn't
made. It probably never was; it wouldn't be easy to actually make
a bed in that oddly shaped space. "Where does your head go?"
she asked, thinking it might be claustrophobic.

"Up in the vee," he said, pointing in that direction. "It's right
beneath the hatch and I can look up at the sky. And when it's
nice I keep the hatch open." Indeed, at the far end of the bunk
an oblique patch of light fell onto the pillows, where, Irene noted,
an orange cat was stretched out in the rumpled bedding.

In the narrow passage they were jammed together, and Irene
suddenly felt trapped, uneasy and distinctly awkward standing
there looking at this man's bed. She made a little motion to
escape. He made himself flat against the wall and lifted his arm

as she ducked past. "It's nice," she said with a quick smile, back in the galley now, not so intimate.

"Thank you," he said. "Can I give you a drink?" When she hesitated he said, "Go up on deck. I'll be right behind you."

Irene did as she was told. Up on the deck the sun had fallen behind the trees on the hills above Route 3, turning the sky a pale violet and throwing the deck into warm shade. She took off her jacket and tugged her tee shirt away from her damp skin. Here she didn't have to hide the gun under her arm—he knew she was carrying. She sat down in one of the lawn chairs and looked out across the water towards Shelton where she could see rafts of logs and the Simpson timber mill sheds and stacks beyond. And beyond that the town climbing up the hill. She wondered if she had her field glasses whether she'd be able to pick out her own house. She could, she thought, see the dock of the Shelton Marina from her upstairs bedroom—the view reversed.

Theo emerged from the galley carrying a bottle of Maker's Mark and a bowl of ice, two glasses hooked in his fingers. He sat down in the other lawn chair and poured them each an inch. "Ditch?" he asked.

She smiled and shook her head. He'd read her right—if she'd wanted water he'd have had to make another trip. His relaxed confidence put her at ease. It was nice there on the deck in the early evening, a little breeze off the water stirring her hair and drying the sweat on the back of her neck. Theo touched the lip of his glass against hers. The bourbon was cold and sharp on her tongue, but the first sip spread a pleasing warmth through her chest.

"Tell me about your case," Theo said.

Irene smiled ruefully. "My case," she said. "It's not going anywhere. I'm going to close it. Call it an accident. There's nothing else to do. It's what the family wants." She looked at him. "I don't think it was an accident, but I don't even have an opinion really about who did it or why, and there's no compelling evidence to support a charge against any one of them."

"A hunch?" he asked.

"A hunch, yes," she agreed. "But I've been in this business long enough to know what I know. I just don't have anything to give you."

In the normal course, if the sheriff's department was going to recommend prosecution, the investigating officer—Irene in this instance—would provide all the reports and evidence relating to the case to the prosecuting attorney's office, and brief Theo too, or whichever assistant was assigned the case, as Irene was doing now, giving him her observations and impressions, details that might not have been captured in anyone's report. The prosecutor relied on the sheriff's department and on the individual officers to provide what was needed for a successful prosecution, and the two departments worked in concert, two branches within the judicial system. If the evidence wasn't there, the prosecutor couldn't prosecute. This was a conversation that was normal and expected in the usual course of business, though it wouldn't typically be taking place after hours over drinks on the deck of someone's boat.

"What are they like," Theo asked after a while, "the Parises?"

"Hmm," said Irene. She liked it that he had asked that question. What *were* they like? "I don't know," she said, "I don't know how to describe them. They're all nice, I guess, in their own way, smart and sophisticated, they're easy to talk to and pleasant enough, and taken one by one I'd have to say they seem just fairly normal and not that much different from you or me or anyone else. No one seems necessarily like they're hiding anything, but then on the other hand there's this sense I have of them closing ranks—like they're gracious and welcoming and they let you in, but only so far and then you hit a wall. They circle the wagons. I think they think they don't have to answer in quite the same way as regular people do to—I don't know what—society? Or Mason County society, maybe. They're their own little fiefdom, their own enclave. They're like aliens in a way, like they landed in a spaceship, or they're from some other culture, just summering out here in the colonies. They have their own standards."

"Entitled," he said.

"Entitled," she agreed, "that's a good word for it." She smiled at him. "And they're accustomed to keeping secrets. They're comfortable keeping stuff to themselves."

After a moment Irene said, "She was very promiscuous, you know, sleeping with a lot of different men."

There was a silence, then Theo said, "And you disapprove?"

Irene felt a sudden flash of pique. She could tell that her cheeks had flushed. "It's an observation, that's all, not a judgment. It's risky behavior." She was quiet for a moment, getting her anger in check, trying to think why she'd said it in the first place and why his comment touched a hot spot. *Did* she disapprove?

"No, I don't disapprove," she said finally, looking at him. "She was very full of life actually, that's the impression I get. She embraced a lot of experiences and that might have gotten her in trouble." To her dismay she felt the prick of tears starting in the back of her eyes. What was *that* about?

Theo leaned forward and placed his hand over hers where it rested on the arm of her chair. Irene went rigid. "I didn't mean to upset you," he said, looking very directly into her eyes. In a moment he removed his hand, sat back and took a sip of his drink, watching her.

Irene was flustered, trying to get a grip. "I'm not upset," she said finally, though she was and she knew he knew it.

They sat in silence for a while, then Irene said, "I've gotten to know her in a way, in the way you do when you're investigating something like this. I'm not sure I would have liked her, but I would like to have known her in life." She paused. "It almost seems as if she could walk through the door at any moment and there she'd be, and I'd know her and be happy to see her. That's what her father said, as if she's just absent, not dead. Anne's become very real to me. I go to the places she's been, I talk to the people she talked to. I've sat on her bed and gone through her dresser drawers. I know a lot about her, but I don't know who killed her. Someone did. She inspired strong feelings in people and for someone it was too much."

Irene wondered if it was the bourbon speaking or if she just needed to have someone to talk to, someone to listen. Sometimes you didn't know what you thought until you said it, like it was all percolating around in your head in a jumble until you actually put it into words. It was one of the downsides to working alone, without a partner. In L.A. in a homicide investigation you'd have an entire team, experts and underlings, all manner of people to talk to, a hurricane of theories and opinions.

She looked at Theo and smiled a little ruefully. "I'm quite obsessed, I guess, at this point. It's all very frustrating."

"Hey, what about me?" he said lightly. "I was looking forward to prosecuting a homicide, inconveniencing the summer folks." He smiled wickedly, lightening the mood. "Are you sure there's nothing?"

"There's nothing," she said, "I'm sure." She ticked them off her fingers. "There's a jilted boyfriend, an angry and envious half-sister, the new secret boyfriend, the angry and envious half-sister's broke and guilty husband—that's one of the men she slept with—and the very assured and manipulative neighbor to the north nursing a crush and a grudge over a property dispute. I can't even rank them in terms of probability. They all had motive, they all had opportunity, but which one is the one that whacked her on the back of the head, I don't know."

Irene was over her pique and feeling calm and relaxed. The cat came up the ladder and brushed against her before jumping onto Theo's crossed legs where it adapted itself like a panther in a tree, limp as silly putty. It was getting dark. Irene should go.

"How's Victor?" Theo asked, sending a little jolt of electricity through Irene's midsection.

"Victor's fine," she said. "I hope you're over that."

"I'm over that," he said.

She threw him a glance from under her eyes. "Thanks," she said softly.

"We'll wait until next time," he added.

"There won't be a next time," she said.

"Okay," he said amiably, "good." Then after a silence, and hesitantly, he asked, "What about that other business?"

Irene didn't want to think about it. She didn't want to be reminded of Patrick McGrath and the incident along Highway 3 or of the presence of Theo Choate on her porch and in her kitchen in the aftermath, the intimacy of his access. The scrapes on her shoulders were healing and the bruising around her eye had mostly faded. She shrugged dismissively. "That's over, too," she said tersely. Then added after a moment, stiffly, a reluctant concession to his concern, "I followed up some afterwards, at the hospital and the department."

"Good," he said simply, letting it go.

"I need to go," she said, and stood up, slipping into her jacket.

He stood up too, dumping the cat unceremoniously onto the deck.

"Thanks for the drink."

"Any time," he said. "Now you know where to find me." He steadied her with a hand as she stepped onto the dock and watched as she picked up the chain and the wad of tape. She flashed him a quick smile, then was gone, walking quickly down the pier into the gathering dusk.

Theo watched her walk away, and he knew she glanced back when she came to the end of the dock before stepping onto the gangway leading up to the parking lot, because her pale hair was the last thing to fade into the darkness and he saw her head turn. He would be silhouetted against the lightness of the water so she'd know he was standing where she'd left him, watching her go. The lines of a song ran through his head, 'I was looking back to see if you were looking back to see If I was looking back to see if you were looking back at me.'

Theo was glad she'd looked but he didn't make too much of it. He still wasn't sure she'd go out with him if he asked. She was jumpy as a cat. Most single women he encountered were on the prowl, dating on Match.com, eager and anxious, their need rendering him cautious and wary. Irene, he thought, wasn't looking at all. In fact she had some sort of invisible fence built up like a force field—he'd felt it when he reached over to touch her hand—that repelled attraction. He wondered again what her story was.

XXIX

nne's body was gone. Released to the mortuary, Chesterine said. The family hadn't wanted anything done, no embalming, nothing cosmetic. They didn't even want her dressed. What was left of Anne was now across the hall in a cardboard coffin in a small private room where the family could congregate and sit for a few minutes before the cremation, which was to take place that afternoon. There would be no service, no pastor, no hymns, no ritual. Rich people are funny, Chesterine had said. Some rich people. They don't care what anyone thinks. "It's practical," she said, "it's all going up in smoke anyway, but some people do more for their pets."

Irene laughed. By now a cardboard coffin and an absence of ceremony seemed to her in keeping with the contradictions of the Paris family and their world—their odd shabby elegance, their quirks, their utter insularity. They did what they felt like doing and set their own bar.

Irene hoped she was doing the right thing, letting the body go. "Well," she said, "that's that."

"That's that," agreed Chesterine. "Sometimes you never know."

"Right," said Irene, thinking of Luis. "I'd like to know."

Chesterine shrugged.

"What's happened with your John Doe suicide?" she asked. "Did they figure that one out?"

"Nope," answered Chesterine, "they're stymied too. Can't ID him." And she laughed, amused by the frustrations bedeviling local law enforcement.

⸻

IN THE hall on her way out, Irene opened a door marked PRIVATE and looked into a dimly lit room where a few rows of chairs on one side faced a coffin opposite. She slipped in, closing the door behind her. A couple of candles gave the room the look of a chapel and a scent of pine. Music was piped in, a tasteful loop of Pachelbel's *Canon*. No offense to anyone. The top half of the coffin was open. It was Anne, her hands folded over a plain shroud, the skin waxy, more like an effigy than a corpse, so little left of life. Irene sat down, tired and dispirited. She leaned forward and crossed her arms on the back of the chair in front of her and rested her head. If anyone looked in, it would appear she was praying. The room was air-conditioned and cold. She'd done what she could. There was plenty for her to move on to, and the seeming importance of the unresolved circumstances of the death of Anne Paris would eventually fade until she wouldn't be able to recall why it had ever seemed to matter.

Her phone was vibrating. "Yes?" she said tersely, sitting back. She knew it was probably not polite to take a call here, but the Parises probably wouldn't care, and anyway, there was no one here to know.

"Hi, honey, I'm home." Ira Logan's voice low and ironic in her ear.

Ira Logan instantly lost his place as Irene's prime suspect and plummeted to the bottom of her list. A wave of relief washed over her. Canada had not swallowed him up after all. She hadn't quite realized just how bad she'd felt about letting him go. She was silent.

"You there?" he asked.

"I'm here," she said.

"It's me, Ira."

"I know," she said.

"I'm back in Boston and I'm packing my things."

"You made good time," Irene said.

"I did," he agreed. "It didn't turn out to be as much fun as I thought. I just wanted to make time. I hardly stopped, hardly slept. But the car ran like a top."

"Where are you going?" she asked.

"I don't know, but I can't stay here. It creeps me out," talking now in his own voice without the irony and sounding a little ragged. "You've been here, right?"

"Right," she agreed.

"Find anything out?" he asked.

"No," she said, "not really."

"What's that supposed to mean?"

"I didn't find anything incriminating or particularly illuminating is what it means," said Irene. She didn't see the point in bringing up what she'd learned about the landlord and his relationship to Anne. "I'm closing the case, calling it an accident."

"You know what's weird?" Ira asked after a moment.

"What?"

"I'm here in our apartment and all I feel is like we've broken up. I don't feel sad like you'd think I would knowing she's dead— I feel bitter and sorry for myself because I've lost her, as if she's left me for someone else. Like she's moved on."

Irene wasn't sure but she thought he was crying. "Ira?" she said.

"I'm taking my clothes and my books and one of the rugs, and I'm leaving the rest."

"Where will you go?" she asked again.

"I don't know. I can live in my car for the time being," he said.

Irene laughed, as he'd meant her to, picturing the Triumph.

"No. I'll put my stuff in storage and stay at the hospital until I find a place. Half the time it feels like I live at the hospital anyway."

Irene thought about telling him where she was at that moment as they were speaking. She imagined putting her phone up against Anne's ear and letting Ira say good-bye. She wondered if she should tell him that the cremation was that afternoon. "Anything I should know?" she asked.

"Not that I know," he said.

"Well," she said.

"Yeah, well," he agreed, "you've got my number."

"And you've got mine."

"Thanks, Detective."

"'Bye, Ira." And they hung up.

So that left Libby and Elliot and Rueben Guevara, because Irene didn't believe that if Ira Logan had whacked Anne on the back of the head, that he would have resurfaced at home in Boston to resume his life and his job and be calling her to check in.

⁂

THE PARIS family was arriving as Irene left. Tall thin figures in dark clothes moving up the walk in the hot afternoon. She passed Oliver on the steps leaning on Libby's arm, wearing a black fedora and a jacket, a muffler folded across his chest despite the heat. He dipped his head but didn't speak, the brim of his hat obscuring his face. She didn't know if she'd been acknowledged or snubbed. Out on the street Leland was parking, the spaces filling in now. Irene saw Rueben Guevara maneuvering his old Lincoln into a spot, and the Strauss brothers without their families coming up the sidewalk. It seemed suddenly very sad and final to Irene, and she wished she'd said something more to Ira. He wouldn't figure in this family anymore.

She wondered what would be said in the little room she'd just vacated, or if they'd say anything at all. She could imagine them sitting in silence, each lost in their own thoughts, until some sign or motion from Oliver indicated that it was time. They'd close the coffin and it would slide through an opening in the wall, where, through a small porthole of thick layers of glass you could watch the flames if you were so inclined. Irene knew—her father had been cremated here. It took a long time. You didn't necessarily expect that. She wondered if the family would stay. She guessed Oliver would, silent and bereft, erect in his chair, waiting for it to be finally and completely over. Waiting to receive a small, heavy container of what had been Anne.

A tow truck had Irene blocked in, delaying her departure. She waited near the street in the shade of the trees watching as the rest of the Paris family and a few friends filed up the walk and disappeared into the somber, rock mortuary.

"Stolen?" she asked the tow truck driver. He was having trouble, the car locked and in park and not a lot of room to maneuver. There was a yellow impound sticker on the windshield—a car parked on a side street, unmoved until someone noticed and called in to the police to report it.

"Not stolen exactly," he answered, "a rental that never got returned. They ran the license plate downtown."

"If you move your truck, I can get out of here and give you some room to maneuver," Irene said. She waited while he backed out of her way, and in the rearview mirror she saw his two-fingered salute as she pulled away. He knew she was a deputy—if he didn't know her, her car gave her away. In fact she knew him too but couldn't remember his name. Scott, maybe. It was probably embroidered on his shirt, but she'd forgotten to look. He'd been with the towing company for years. He'd have an easier time now.

⚜

Back in her office it was hard to concentrate. Irene began assembling all the papers and reports cluttering her desk that related to Anne Paris. She'd consolidate it all into a file and it would go into storage, a closed case. At some point, the documents would be photographed and everything would be stored on microfiche—or scanned, if the county budgeted for the technology—the hard copies destroyed.

Unpinning the photo montage from her wall, she still wondered what she had missed, if there was something she hadn't noticed or had failed to register as important. Irene was reminded of the movie *Blowup*, which she'd seen years before in re-release, a paean to the power of photography and what a camera might capture in a seemingly innocuous frame.

Who had smoked the cigarette, she wondered, looking at the image of her own two boots and the butt between them, and when? There was no way to tell if it had been the night that Anne died or the night before or the night before that. It was a Marlboro, not a Camel Light, the brand everyone else who smoked seemed to smoke. The grass was trampled, suggesting that someone had stood there restlessly for a while, looking at the slough beyond the plums and rushes—or looking up through the orchard towards the house?—then crushed out the finished cigarette. Not the cigarette that Ira smoked on the beach, and not the cigarette that Julian Bernstein saw lit as he walked away along the beach. An inland cigarette, smoked by whom?

In one of the photos taken from the beach that showed the Guevara house in the background, Irene now—with the benefit of her increased familiarity—could faintly make out a figure she hadn't noticed before, just a dark pattern against the French doors that opened onto the porch, positioned as if looking toward the slough. Rueben Guevara, Irene thought, his attention drawn by her presence on the beach that morning or by the approaching sirens or perhaps by his knowledge of what was floating in the slough. She wondered if he had put the body there or had already discovered it through his telescope or on an early morning walk, and then had watched the unfolding scene. He hadn't mentioned being aware of anything prior to his interview conducted that day. He was a wily one.

The photos brought back the day—the clear skies and the promise of heat, Rosalie nattering on and on, the body that Irene didn't yet know was Anne Paris rocking gently at the edge of the slough. It seemed like a long time ago, but it was only days.

Irene unpinned the photos and accordioned them into unruly stacks. She would like to have left them up for a while, but they were part of the record of the case and should be filed with the rest.

Verizon had produced a record of the calls Anne's cell phone had sent and received over the two weeks preceding her death, and Irene had matched up the numbers with names. Not many calls and no surprises. Anne was on vacation and cell reception was spotty. The Atkins Hospital was on the list, both Storey Lindstrom's office number and a landline on the ward—the patient, Irene presumed, who was missing his therapist before he went missing himself—and Anne calling her own office, for messages, she supposed. There were calls to and from Julian Bernstein's cell phone and two calls from a pay phone in Shelton—an artifact from another civilization—Irene wondered how many pay phones even existed anymore. Julian Bernstein had said he'd called from Shelton once when he was in town and couldn't get a cell signal, but only once, he was pretty sure. Same number, same phone, outside of the Safeway store, the evening Anne died. So the second call—if not Julian, who then?

Everyone's typed-up interview and the follow-up interviews, the medical examiner's report, the coroner's report, lists of evidence collected, lists of confiscated personal property, search warrants, interrogation reports—it was all there, a paper trail of the law enforcement effort to ascertain how Anne Paris's body had come to be in the slough at the bottom of her family's summer property.

XXX

Something was bothering Irene. There was something in the back of her mind, like a forgotten appointment, something she was supposed to have done. It was making her jumpy and uneasy. She was going home, she decided. It was early to quit, but she'd been working long days and hadn't had a weekend. She'd run, she thought, run now, early, before dusk. It would be like getting back on the horse, facing down her fear, and she'd feel better afterwards. It would clear her head.

Wanda glanced at the clock as Irene walked past. Inspector Gilbert was going to get an earful when he got back from vacation. Irene would be called on the carpet and asked for an accounting. Oh, well, she thought, she'd be hard to fire and she doubted he'd try. Besides, she had no apologies for her comings and goings.

Victor's bike was at the market when she passed, and she angled into a parking spot and went in. She picked up some chicken to grill, and leeks and peppers and a couple of ears of corn. At the checkout, while Victor was bagging the groceries, she told him she'd throw it all on the grill after her run and a shower, and when would he be home. She was taking tomorrow off, she told him, and she'd drive him down to Olympia if he wanted, to look at the bicycle he was interested in. When Victor smiled, she saw Luis—the same sweet dazzle, white teeth, crinkled eyes.

"Cool," he said.

Irene was off-kilter and needed to get her equilibrium back. Supper with Victor and errands with him tomorrow would help.

⟡

IT WAS really bad déjà vu. She was passing under the Simpson sluiceway and could see the log rafts below and smell the pitch, when a vehicle came up from behind and slowed beside her, the rumble of a diesel engine. She was afraid to look and kept running, her eyes straight ahead. It was daylight, nothing could happen. Keep running, stay calm. The vehicle kept pace. She refused to look. Then it sped up and pulled past her—a black Ford pickup, not new, not Patrick McGrath's she didn't think. Then it swerved into a wide spot on the shoulder, blocking her path. She slowed, panting, her heart flipping in her chest. The same spot as before, Irene thought, panic rising. She had her phone with her this time, clipped to the waistband of her shorts. The driver's door swung open—she was poised to sprint in the opposite direction. But it was Theo Choate swinging out, wearing a suit, his tie loosened.

"Irene," he said, approaching her.

She gasped, her hand on her heart, eyes wide.

He reached to touch her shoulder and she jerked away. She was starting to cry. She stood with her back to him, shoulders shaking, her face in her hands, trying to regain control.

Finally she turned and faced him. "You *scared* me," she blurted, her face flushed, cheeks wet. He reached for her and this time she let him enfold her in his arms.

"I didn't mean to," he whispered into her hair. "You scared *me*, out here on the highway by yourself." For just a moment he felt her relax against him, pliant and supple, fitting her slim hot body into his, and he felt the sweat on her neck and the wet back of her shirt under his hand, before she gathered herself and pulled away.

He released her. "You want a ride back?" he asked.

She shook her head. "No," she said, exhaling, "It's good for me. I need the run." She took a deep breath, looked at her watch, flung him a glance, and was off—running away, passing his pickup, heading north again with the same steady rhythm.

Theo got back in his truck, but he waited. It took six minutes, and then there she was again, headed back. She dodged past the truck with barely a glance—he might not have existed. He watched her in the rearview mirror until she disappeared.

⁂

SOMETHING HAD shaken loose in Irene's mind. Something to do with assumptions. She was having trouble putting her finger on it. It was the pickup, thinking it was Patrick McGrath, thinking she was in danger—an assumption based on experience, thinking based on symmetry, if it was Patrick McGrath before, it will be Patrick McGrath again—when really it was almost the opposite, Theo Choate this time, looking out for her, worrying about her safety, almost her guardian actually. And she hadn't pictured Theo Choate in a pickup, just as she hadn't pictured him on a boat. She'd assumed something else from the education and the suit and the self-possession. A Saab maybe. Assumptions were not a detective's friend. You had to keep your mind blank and accumulate facts. Truth was always in the facts. Collect enough facts, you learn the truth. You didn't weigh facts, rank their importance, you just collected them. But human nature got in the way, what you knew about human nature and your own human nature, the desire for logic, for one thing to follow another, for patterns, for symmetry. As in poker you discarded, threw out the club when the rest of the hand was hearts, working on a flush. She was thinking as she ran. Trying to think outside the box, to cast a wider net—trying to reclaim her discards.

⁂

WHEN SHE came back into town, Irene didn't head up the hill towards home and the groceries she'd bought and the promised supper, but instead made a right onto Railroad Street and ran along the tracks, past the vintage Burlington Northern engine installed out in front of the post office for kids to climb on, past the J. C. Penney's store where her mother had worked—now a Good Shepherd thrift store with a hand-painted sign in the window SI HABLA ESPAÑOL—and on to the outskirts of town to where the Shelton Police Station was backed up against the hill behind a gravel parking lot.

The watch sergeant on duty was Hoyt Brenner. He had been a town cop as long as Irene could remember—he'd pulled her over and ticketed her for a California stop when she was a teenager. A good cop, not too much attitude, kept his head down and got the job done. He was way past where he could have retired and there was no way he would pass the physical agility test, so they kept him pretty much on the desk. He watched her walk in and head directly for the water cooler. She downed a cup of water and several refills, and then went into the visitor's bathroom and splashed water on her face. She was flushed and drenched in sweat. When she came out, Hoyt was waiting for her, smiling pleasantly. She leaned her elbows on his counter.

"Hey, Hoyt," she said.

"Hey," he said, "how goes it?"

"Fine," she said, "good." She was getting her breath back, radiating an aura of heat.

"You on duty?" he asked.

Irene laughed. "No, off," she said. "Out for a run. But hey, I'm here on business. I've got a question."

"Shoot," he said.

"You guys impounded a car this afternoon, a rental that wasn't returned?"

"Yup."

"Who was the renter?"

Hoyt shuffled through a pile of papers on his desk until he found what he was looking for. "Guy who rented it is Jan Guyot,

G-u-y-o-t, according to the Budget records. Picked it up at Sea-Tac Saturday before last on a two-day rental and never came back. There's nothing in the computer, no record, no warrant, no missing person."

"Home address?"

"Don't have it. We just ran the tag and let them know we had their car, and ran the name and driver's license they gave us for warrants."

"Have you gotten inside?"

"Haven't tried. Budget's sending someone with a key in the morning. We'll take a look before we let it go."

"Let me know what you find, would you?" asked Irene.

"Will do," said Hoyt. He wasn't even curious—too many years on the job.

⁂

IRENE LEFT, calculating the time difference—past ten on the east coast. She had Storey Lindstrom in her cell phone. It took him a while and there was noise in the background when he answered. It sounded like a bar or a restaurant. He was out somewhere, enjoying his evening. She knew nothing about him, she realized, nothing about his personal situation. She tried to remember if he'd worn a ring. She thought she would have noticed.

"Dr. Lindstrom," she said, "Irene Chavez."

"I'm sorry?" he shouted. "Hello?"

"Irene Chavez," she yelled back, "out in Washington State?"

"Oh, sure," he said, hearing her now, "how are you?"

"I'm fine," she said. "Listen, the patient of Anne's you told me about who went missing—what was his name?"

"The what—oh, Jan Guyot."

"Bingo," she said.

"What?" he shouted.

"Nothing," she said. "I'll call you tomorrow. It's too hard to talk now."

XXXI

One last time Irene's Crown Victoria glided down the driveway through the tunnel of trees and rolled to a stop in the blinding light and heat shimmer between the buildings of the Paris family compound. The place had become familiar—the purple spires of foxgloves nodding in the heat and the espaliered pear against the barn, the disheveled rose climbing the porch trellis to the upstairs windows, scenting the yard with its fragrance, the peeling white paint and silvered siding of the barn. But for Irene, even now, every time, it retained the surreal quality of the first time—a feeling of having jumped down the rabbit hole and entered an alternative universe where she lost herself and who she was in normal life, and where she was dazed and out of step, uncharacteristically uncertain.

She opened the car door and got out. It was hot under a pale sky. Irene walked across the expanse of bleached grass toward the bluff. There was no sign of life—no curtain lifted, no one sitting in the Adirondack chairs and no one at the table or rattling dishes in the kitchen. If there was someone watching from behind the reflection in the glass of the study windows, Irene couldn't tell.

She stood looking out at the still water of the Sound for a few moments, the metallic surface disturbed here and there as a breeze she didn't feel but could hear high in the firs touched down.

She turned then and crossed the yard again and stepped up onto the porch of the study and rapped smartly on the door and waited. Nothing. She pushed the door open and looked in to be sure. Empty.

She walked on past the barn—vacant—and on down the orchard path toward the beach. The lanes between the lichen-hung trees were neatly mown. Just in time for the end of summer and the Parises' departure, Irene thought, marveling again at the sheer insanity of it—Libby's self-imposed penance for some imagined transgression, or maybe her noisy, masochistic way of making sure her father knew she was earning her keep, out there doing a hard day's labor while the rest of them read and sailed and pursued more refined pastimes. Libby was a hornet in the family, riling things up, keeping everyone on edge. But she had not killed her sister, of this Irene was certain.

At the bottom of the orchard, when she could see the slough and the vista beyond, Irene was arrested—out beyond the slough, out on the dune, silhouetted under a milky sky, the Paris family was incongruously arranged on the beach, all in black, still as chessmen, all turned toward Oliver Paris, hatless on the crest of the dune, one arm dipping and waving as though conducting or orating.

The ashes, Irene realized, seeing the plume following his hand, spreading Anne's ashes. She stood where she was, transfixed by the spectacle.

High in the firs somewhere behind her an eagle whistled. A glint of light flashed across the corner of her eye and she jerked her head—the telescope of course, Rueben Guevara positioned in the window of his living room, trespassing still, participating unseen in the Paris family's private ritual—a reflection bouncing momentarily off the lens as he panned the slough and turned the focus on Irene. Eyes everywhere. Here, on Gustavus Island where you thought you were invisible, thought you could pee in the woods unseen, make love on the beach, break and enter, there was no telling who was watching.

Out on the dune Oliver Paris had become still, his arm hanging limp at his side, the canister empty. As Irene watched he took his hat from under his elbow and clamped it firmly onto his head, a decisive tug to the brim. The breeze was teasing the ends of his muffler. The little group shifted, turning away, beginning to move toward the path, their dark clothing flapping in the pale afternoon. The weather, Irene thought, was changing.

Libby's boys, released, ran the length of a driftwood log, one behind the other, and jumped. Irene heard them shout. Phoebe slid off Rosie's hip and followed her cousins.

⁂

IRENE WAS here for the last time and she had come to tell the Paris family what had befallen Anne. She knew now what had happened, though she couldn't prove it. There would be no arrest. But she had put it together with as much certainty as she'd ever felt about anything. She'd been on the right track from the start, her instincts good—it was just as she had suggested to Dr. Paris— Anne, loved by everyone, was loved too much.

⁂

THE NIGHT of the squall, the night of Anne's death, after the storm had passed and darkness had fallen, there was a lot of traffic along the orchard path to the beach.

First came the trespasser, his car left up on the road, pulled inconspicuously into a trailhead above the mailboxes. He had Google map directions for guidance, but he didn't walk down the driveway. Instead he ducked into the wet underbrush and pushed his way through the band of woods between the Paris property and the Guevara's until he emerged into the orchard behind the barn, soaked to the waist. He stood at the edge of the orchard while his eyes adjusted to the ambient light. Then he advanced, stopping first beside the abandoned outhouse tilting under a canopy of climbing wild rose. He pushed open the latticework door and stepped into the narrow, dark space and lit a cigarette, sitting on the closed privy lid, listening and looking out at the orchard rows and at the lit windows of the Paris house visible through the branches. Unused for many years, there was no odor other than the fragrance of the rose and the lingering pleasant scent of cut grass wafting from the orchard. The hinges squealed when he stepped out again.

He continued down through the apple trees, a commando darting from trunk to trunk, to where Irene now stood.

Here, within the scrim of wild plum and reeds, he was hidden from the house, hidden should anyone approach along the path, and camouflaged should anyone look in his direction from the beach. From here, where he stood smoking another cigarette, he could see the canoe tied up to the buoy and he would have known that Anne was still out with the boat.

He waited, standing in the dark listening to the wind, full of excitement and anticipation.

Later still—the trespasser has grown weary and agitated, nothing worse than waiting, nothing harder on the soul, nothing more dispiriting, more anger-inducing. He has pushed through the huckleberry and salal that crowd the path to the beach and has emerged into a tangle of driftwood. He sits on a log looking out at the water. He's watching for a sail. But his earlier exhilaration is waning.

Then noises, someone approaching, footfalls on the orchard path. The trespasser's spirits soar. He has been watching for a boat, expecting to see, far out where there is still some wind, the ghost of a sail. It has gotten late. He stands up in anticipation and almost steps forward to welcome and accost. But wait! There are two people coming. Two sets of footfalls, two shapes in the darkness blending into one as they emerge onto the beach. He stays where he is and watches them. He has been waiting there a long time by now and his eyes are animal eyes, accustomed to the dark, and he knows what he sees. It's Anne. The glint of her hair and he can hear her voice in the timbre of her breath. He waits. They pass close by. They lean together. They kiss. She murmurs something. Then they move past him onto the dune. Just yards away. If they looked, they could see him. He hasn't ducked or hidden. He's standing among the logs, frozen. The reality of what is unfolding is so at variance with his imagination—her delight and welcome when she discovers him, and their embrace—*their* embrace.

As he watches, she slips out of her jacket and lets it drop behind her onto the sand. She tugs her shorts down and he can see her pale belly, the dark triangle before she sinks down, opening her legs. The man is standing above her, loosening his trousers. Then he kneels and the trespasser can see her legs lift and wrap around him as he bends over her. He can hear them pant—surely they will hear *his* breathing, he's choking, can't get enough air. His mind has gone blank, his head exploding. He hears Anne's cry of pleasure.

He wonders if he's fainted. There's been a time lapse, he's missed something. The man is walking away and Anne is standing and he is moving and the stick of wood in his hand is swinging and he hears the crack and feels the concussion and he sees her flying sideways, knocked off her feet, falling away from him. He hears the thud as she lands and the soft splash as she rolls into the slough.

⌘

ONCE, WHEN things were very bad, he killed his cat. He loved his cat, loved it more than anything, his sole solace, the warm treasured presence at night, the pleased greeting at each return. His cat was part of himself, like a limb or an ear. Anne had said he must stop his cutting—his target behavior—replace it somehow to avoid harming himself.

So when the need to cut got very strong he picked up the cat and buried his face in its soft, warm fur and carried it into the bathroom where he shoved it into the toilet bowl and sat down on the lid, flushing over and over, listening to the rush of water and feeling the frantic thrashing of the cat, waiting for a long time while it howled and scrabbled and became weak and finally drowned and was silent. He felt hideous and exquisite pain, but he endured it, thinking that afterwards there would be peace, but there wasn't. Afterwards the cat was no longer there to comfort him. The cat was a limp rag of wet fur that had stopped up his plumbing. The toilet bowl had overflowed and he vomited into the sink. He ripped off his shirt and cut himself savagely. He sank to the floor, wedged between the tub and the toilet.

He called and Anne came. She cancelled a patient and was there inside of twenty minutes and found him on the bathroom floor in a sodden mess of blood and fur and water. She lifted him up and held him and wound towels around his arms, and he wrapped his arms around her and felt her warm thinness through her clothes. He tried to kiss her but she whispered, "No, no, we mustn't. We have to get you better first. We have work to do."

He let her lead him to her car and drive him to Atkins where she said he would be safe and he couldn't hurt himself or anyone and she would be there. It was intimate in her car, warm and messy. There was a bottle of vitamin water in the cup holder and turkey jerky on the dashboard, file folders on the floorboards. It smelled of peanuts and cigarettes. She drove fast, leaning forward, braking and accelerating, dodging lane to lane, hurrying.

⚜

HE CHECKED himself in and they did the work together. He was getting better. She guided him gently. She understood him and didn't judge. They met every day. Alone in her office at the hospital and twice a week in group. She was always so pleased to see him. "Hello," she said softly, "please, come in," opening the door in welcome. He knew she looked forward to their fifty-minute hours as much as he did. The high point of each day. She looked at him with such kindness and warmth every time they met, always intensely curious about how he was doing, what he was thinking, how he had fared since their last meeting. He knew she loved him. She gave him hints and clues. He could call her any time, night or day, and she'd answer. He didn't call her often, but enough to reassure himself it was true. She always answered or quickly phoned him back. She let him touch her, she let him take her hand, hold it sometimes while they talked, leaning forward in the two facing chairs. He knew that they were only waiting until he was better. When he was strong enough they would be together.

But then she left him alone at Atkins with a substitute therapist. Abandoned him. It was August and she told him she was going on vacation. She told him where she was going and when she'd be back. She told him about the sailboat and swimming in the cold water, about the woods and the beach. She wanted him to be able to picture her in her absence. She wanted him to know that she was still present in the world, though absent for the moment from his, out on the other coast, but seeing the same moon that rose above his horizon. She said she knew it would be hard and she expected he would be angry and lonesome, but she would be back and they would resume, and he could call her if he needed to. He had her cell phone number.

What she didn't tell him is that it would be intolerable. It wasn't hard, it was impossible. He couldn't endure it. And so he followed her.

⬥

It's NOT much later. Only moments have passed. The trespasser has leaped down the shoulder of the dune in a shower of sand and has splashed into the slough beside Anne, rolling her over, turning her face up, fingers feeling for a pulse beneath her jaw, bending to put his mouth against hers, to breathe life into her, cradling her head in his hand. But under his palm on the back of her head is a spongy crater and he pushes her away, sickened, knowing she is dead. Now he is sitting in the reeds near her body. He's wet and cold and someone else is coming down through the orchard.

It's Ira, passing nearby on his way to the beach to smoke his night-time cigarette. The trespasser hears his approach and watches without moving. He's totally numb, his mind no longer works.

Ira emerges onto the beach and stands on the dune looking out at the Sound. He too notes the canoe on the buoy, and feels a prickle of anxiety, knowing Anne has taken the I-14 and has not returned. He lights a cigarette. He wonders if there is something wrong and if there is something he should do. He thinks too about the car he's working on, what he'll tackle tomorrow. He wonders if what has gone wrong between him and Anne is fixable. He thinks about the work at the hospital in Boston he'll soon return to. He thinks about the Ecuadorian girl. He sits down on a driftwood log and watches the constellations emerge behind the broken clouds as the storm moves south, thinking himself alone with his thoughts, while all the while behind him the trespasser watches from the edge of the slough; and behind *him*, up the hill, through the lens of his telescope, Rueben Guevara has seen the match flare and the ash glow on the end of the cigarette; and some distance down the beach Julian Bernstein has turned to look back, and waves in the darkness, imagining it is Anne lighting a cigarette on the dune while she watches him depart.

⊰◈⊱

SOMETIME IN the night the trespasser clambers out of the slough and returns to his car, pushing through thickets and underbrush, and drives himself off the island and back to the motel in Shelton where, in another lifetime, cagy then, and optimistic, he had rented a room, using an amusing alias in case his parents or someone from Atkins or anyone else came looking for him.

He parks on a side street, slips into the motel room and lies down on the bed in the dark, shivering in his wet clothes despite the heat.

It's nearly dawn before he cuts himself. This time he doesn't hold back. The razor goes deep in the soft underside of his wrist and he draws it slowly upward through years of scars, watching the blood spurt. The other side is harder, he's already weak.

⊰◈⊱

Now, IRENE realized, was the wrong moment to try to talk to the family. Her timing was off. And she didn't want to be discovered here, watching, an uninvited guest intruding on a family affair. She turned and slipped into the orchard and walked hurriedly up the hill among the trees so as not to be seen.

It didn't matter, she thought. They didn't want to know. They were content to go on not knowing. But she knew. She had put it all together and she had come out to Gustavus Island one last time to tell them, to tell Oliver Paris and the rest of them so they'd know. 'Closure,' in the vocabulary of grief. Now, interestingly, the knowing didn't seem so important. It was important to her—she was a good detective and it mattered to her that she'd figured it out and wasn't filing something unfinished—but in the scheme of things it didn't seem terribly important. Telling them now, or ever, seemed prideful and unnecessary, more about her than about them. And it seemed oddly and disappointingly improbable that she hadn't put it all together sooner. One random bit of information, seemingly unrelated, holding the key to it all— 'John Doe suicide,' Chesterine had said, 'Soundview Motel. The cops have it.'

⁂

SHE'D GRILLED that evening after her run, and told Victor that she was working the next day after all. She was on a case, she'd had a break and had to follow up. She thought he understood, and if he was disappointed, he didn't let it show. It had happened before.

Later though, after they had eaten, he said, "I could take the bus."

Irene thought this over. "But how would you get it home if you bought it?"

"The commuter bus has a bike rack."

She wondered if he'd researched this—growing up, finding his own solutions. She was reluctant, she didn't really know why, but she had said okay and Victor had smiled and said cool.

The next morning she was there when the man from Budget showed up to collect the car. Jan Guyot had left his wallet and his meds and his phone and his carry-on in the car. It was haste, Irene figured, rather than a deliberate attempt for anonymity. A positive ID was made and Chesterine notified the family. Budget took the car. Irene called Atkins. Storey Lindstrom was badly shaken and didn't want to get off the phone. He'd pulled the file and had read Anne's notes overnight and was blaming himself. He hoped there wouldn't be a suit.

Irene wrote her report. Anne's death would be filed: homicide/suicide, case closed. There was already a message on her desk from a reporter for the *Mason County Journal*. There would be a torrid story in the paper about the summer residents, full of innuendo and inaccuracy and supposition, but by then the Paris family would be gone.

Leland would pull Oliver's ancient Mercedes into the barn, set it up on blocks, drain the radiator and disconnect the battery. The canoe and the Adirondack chairs would be carried into the barn; and in the house, sheets thrown over the beds and furniture, the floors swept and shades drawn, awaiting another summer.

⟣

At the junction with Highway 3 Irene's phone vibrated. "Chavez," she said. It was Theo Choate blurting out an invitation. Was she free Friday and would she let him take her to dinner? "What's today?" she asked, and he laughed. Then she said yes, thank you, she would like that, and they hung up. "Oh, my," she said aloud, and flipped the visor and looked up and met her own startled eyes in the vanity mirror.

Her radio crackled to life. The joint operation with the Kitsap detectives had paid off and they were moving in, calling for backup. Irene hit the gas and her grill lights and swung north, on to other things.

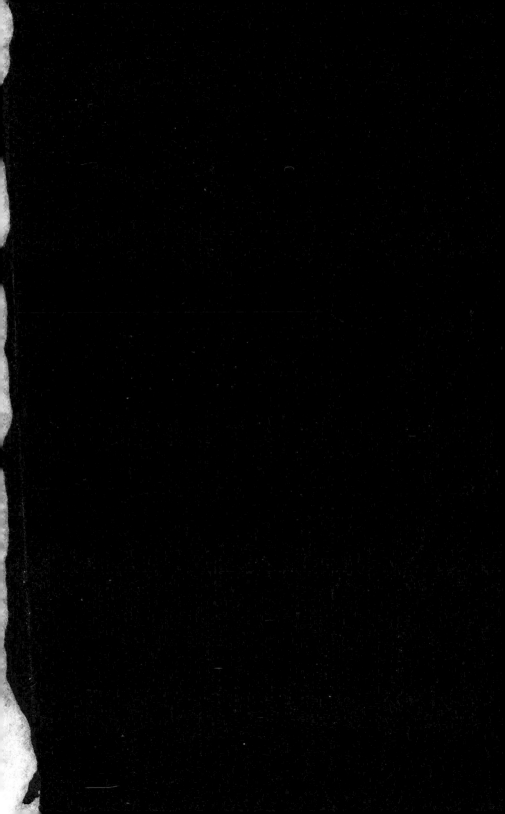